SECRETS OF CONFESSIONS AND MORE STORIES

Benjamín Guillén Corona

America Star Books
Frederick, Maryland

© 2015 by America Star Books.

All rights reserved. No part of this book may be reproduced, stored in a retrieval system or transmitted in any form or by any means without the prior written permission of the publishers, except by a reviewer who may quote brief passages in a review to be printed in a newspaper, magazine or journal.

First printing

All characters in this book are fictitious, and any resemblance to real persons, living or dead, is coincidental.

Softcover 9781681223186
PUBLISHED BY AMERICA STAR BOOKS, LLLP
www.americastarbooks.pub
Frederick, Maryland

DEDICATION

Again I'd like to thank infinitely my father God. I really feel proud and blessed to have received the great gift of inspiration

My parents Francisco Guillen Jaramillo and Edilberta Corona Zavala. They are the motor in my life, Panchito and Edi, I LOVE YOU!!

To all my family in general, it's impossible for me to name them one by one. I'd need not one but many books. From the bottom of my heart I thank you for your unconditional love and support. Seeing the faith you guys have in me makes me feel more confident than ever, I know I don't always say it but I love you so much! I am so proud to be part of such a great family!

To all my friends, you know who you are. Thank you so much for always being there and for showing me how proud you are of me. I'm also proud of you all and I have you in my heart.

To my nieces, Jessica Reyes Torres and Edith Yesenia Guillen Estrada, (I love you sweeties) thank you so much for all your invaluable help in this book.

To America Star Books, thank you for giving me the opportunity to realize my dream, your support is invaluable to me.

For you…YOU KNOW WHO YOU ARE…Thank you so much for motivating me to want to be a better man…I LOVE YOU *CCR!!

Finally, I'd like to thank you, the one holding this book. It is an honor that you would dedicate some of your time to reading my stories. Your support inspires me to be better.

Please remember this:
Dreams come true when you put all your effort into them. If dreaming doesn't scare you, maybe you're not dreaming big enough!

Benjamin Guillen Corona
(Sagid)

FOREWORD

Priests are common and ordinary just like us all. The difference is that they are prepared and consecrated to the service of God and the people. We have a tendency of forgetting that they are also men.

They are obligated to keep secret everything we confess to them. Their duty is to give his forgiveness and help us repent, but, how willing is a priest to keep our secrets, what about when the confession affects him personally, what about when it hurts him?

"In my studies at the seminary they never prepared me for a confession like this…How am I to give absolution to this man?"

This is how one of my writings begins in Secrets of Confession

I dare you to try and put yourself in the shoes of priest and tell me,

In his place, would you?

One more thing…

Let yourself get submerged in these stories that will touch your heart, they're going to surprise you with the unexpected endings…

INTRODUCTION

In Spanish, when we go to confess, the priest ask us, Ave Maria Purisima? (HAIL MARY FULL OF GRACE) and we answer him, Sin pecado Concebido (WITHOUT SIN CONCEIVED) but in English people said, "Bless me Father for I have sinned. It has been…since my last confession. There is nothing particular that the priest says to start.

This book was written in Spanish and translated into English, this is the reason why you will find some words and customs in Spanish.

When a is seen coin on the ground, one person may analyze the value of the coin, another will probably observe to see which face is up, someone else might analyze how dirty it is, someone else might pick it up and stick it in her pocket.

What I try to get you to understand with this, is that we all see things from different perspectives.

Rape, crime, incest, betrayal, lies, ambition, pedophilia

I only some of them sins people commit on the daily.

How many of you have asked yourself how a priest must feel, think, and want to act when these things are confessed to him and make him feel involved?

Secrets of Confession, is a book that tells stories about situations that are out of the ordinary, that unfold unexpected and unpredictable events but that without a doubt show you the many faces of a person.

I invite you, to read this book with an open mind and heart.

INDEX

DEDICATION 3
FOREWORD 5
INTRODUCTION 7

THE RAPE 11
THE MURDERER 15
CYBER CONNECTION 20
SENTENCED TO DEATH 25
THE CANDYMAN 29
THE PEDOPHILE 33
CONCEIVED WITHOUT SIN 38
MATRICIDE 43
IN BETWEEN DUTY AND LIFE 48
THE SURPRISE 54
INCEST 58

THE WRITER FROM HELL (FOREWORD) 62
* THE WRITER OF HELL * 63
SOMETHING MORE 77
CHILD FULL OF GRACE 78
GOD'S TELEPHONE NUMBER 81
THE GRADUATION 83
WITHERED ROSES 89
KAPLAN 94
HERO 99
ALX 105
OH, MY AUGUSTINE! 109
WITNESS 114
PROCESSION 118
RUN! 122
EL CACHITO (THE LOTTERY TICKET) 130
VIRGEN FOR SALE 133
THE WRITER 136

MEMORY	141
UNTIL I WANT TO	145
HUG	150
TRUE LOVE	154

THE RAPE

It was extremely painful to perform the funeral rites. It had been one of the most challenging things I had to do in my short time as a priest.

Her body lies in the coffin. She was covered so people would not see her beat up and disfigured face. That angelic face and made her worthy of being crowned queen of our festival.

She had just started living her life. Had so many dreams, I remember her telling me that she wanted to be a social worker, so she'd be able to help the many women and children that are mistreated.

After her Christian burial, I went to the temple to pray. I needed to be alone before returning to my parish. The bishops suggested that I take a few days off to be with my family, but there is too much to be done in a parish so I decided to return today.

I was looking up at our Lord on the cross when I heard footsteps coming from behind. I figured it was someone that wanted pray. So I stood to make room.

"Wait father" said the voice of a man, "I need to confess myself, do you have time to listen?"

The last thing I wanted to do was hear other people's sins right now. But the man's face looked haggard, he had dark circles around his eyes, you could tell he hadn't slept well for days. He must've been on 22 years of age, I decided to listen to his confession.

"Of course my son, follow me."

We enter the confessional room and I prepare myself to listen to his confession.

"Hail Mary full of Grace" he remained without responding for a while.

"Father I need you to help me the remorse is killing me…"

"Is your sin that bad, son?"

"It's very bad, I don't know with the start."

"Calm down son, our Lord is infinitely merciful and he will forgive you regardless of what your sin is."

"Last Friday in the afternoon my friends called me to go have some drinks with them at a bar. I didn't really feel like going because when I drink I tend to lose myself control and I act as if I was a different person but they insisted and I couldn't say no.

We went to a bar near here, we drank a lot. Around 9 PM we decided to go elsewhere to find something fun to do. We rode in one of my friends vehicles, we had only driven a few blocks when we saw a beautiful girl.

"Hey princess, why so lonely?" said my friend Ismael.

The girl turned around but didn't say anything, it was evident she got a little scared and started walking quicker.

"How about we take her for a ride with us?" said my friend Victor.

"Whoever is too coward to do it will get his butt kicked. What do you say Arturo?" asked Pedro.

"Let's do it" I respond.

We got off the car, immediately she started running. We quickly caught her and we put her in the car. She tried to fight back, but it was four of us against one she was defenseless. We took her to an alley behind the supermarket and raped her.

I was first, she tried to hit me, so I struck her in the face. This way she would stay still, my friends held her hands and feet to make it easier for me.

Next was Victor, it bothered him a lot that she kept fighting back so he started beating her without mercy. It felt like I was dreaming at this point because the alcohol started to haze my brain.

Ismael and Pedro also beat her a lot while they return. All she could to at this point was moan, she lost all strength to defend herself.

Once we were done and dressed. I saw how she was bleeding from everywhere. We quickly got in the car and got out of there as quickly as we could leaving her behind.

Fortunately for us no one saw us, we agreed to never speak of the subject to anyone.

Two days ago I read on the newspaper that she died.

Since then I haven't been able to sleep. The remorse is killing me. I'd like to say the truth, talk to her family or turn myself into the authorities but I'm scared to go to jail. I've heard of the things they do to rapist in there, aside from that I'm worried that something may happen to my parents because of my fault.

Please, help me...what should I do father?"

Tears ran down my face the whole time I listened to the confession of this rapist. I could imagine everything perfectly, I could clearly see her begging for help, I can see her face covered in blood and tears. Abandoned, alone, in pain.

Why did they do this to her?

Why did they just leave her to die after raping her?

Why?

With a broken voice I say,

"Her name was Christina. She had big dreams and aspirations, you and your friends made sure that now they'll never come to be. She was a defenseless girl who didn't hurt anyone. She dreamt of becoming a professional and helping others. She was only 17 years old, she was an exceptional daughter and friend and...

MY SISTER!

THE MURDERER

My seminary studies never prepared me for a confession like this…

How can I give this man absolution?

It's been two months since I was ordained as a priest. I was assigned as vicar to Father Vidal to the parish of San Juan Diego to get some experience. This way I could later on be assigned to one of the many parishes in Diocese of Valle de Chalco.

Valle de Chaclo, where I was born, raised, and where I lost my parents.

Valle de Chaclo, the place I left many years ago.

I never thought that the bishop would send me to the exercise my ministry to the city where I had so many sad and painful memories. The Lord's paths are unfathomable and if it's his will for me to serve in my home town then so be it.

My schedule to hear confessions is from 7 to 9 at night. It's a quarter till nine and I'm eager to go to the sacristy where I can take off my cassock and meet with father Vidal for dinner. We need to discuss the details for the upcoming Festival.

I looked down at my watch, which was a gift for my grandparents the day that I was ordained as a priest. I begin to pray in silence and ask and no one else comes to confess. My prayer isn't heard, I hear someone come in for confession.

"Hail Mary full of Grace"

Silence

I repeat, "Hail Mary full of Grace"

Silence.

After hearing no response again. I ask, "is there something I can help you with?"

A barely audible male voice says, "I have sinned father, I'm a killer."

"What did you say?" My voice is shaky

"I am a killer…I killed a couple"

"I beg your pardon? You killed a couple?" I can't help how shaky my voice is.

"Yes father, everything happened a little over 20 years ago. 20 years…I've kept quiet all this time, but the remorse is killing me, there's not one night that I can sleep soundly. As soon as I close my eyes I see their faces father. I'm desperate for forgiveness from God."

Then he tells me the details

"Since the first time I saw her at the market, I began to follow her. I had never seen such a beautiful woman, everyone admired her beauty. Her face reflected happiness and she had the body of a goddess. I tried asking her out but she told me that she was married. I became obsessed like I had never been with anyone else, and he swore to myself that she would be mine whatever the cost.

I found out what her name was and where she lived. I practically became her shadow. I followed her at all times of the day, I became friends with hers which is how I found out that she'd be celebrating her seventh wedding anniversary. That she'd be going out for dinner with her husband and leaving her son Ricardo, who was 5 at the time, with the neighbor. It felt like the perfect opportunity to carry out my plan…"

"Did you say her son's name was…"

"Father please, I must finish…"

As he continues to narrate the details, I see the images in my head and feel air constricted.

"They had dinner in Tlahuac, The town that's about 20 minutes from here, at Los Arcos restaurant. On their way to the bus stop they had to walk through a dark road. I waited for them, I had a sharp knife with me.

They were holding hands, laughing, happy, and talking about what a good time they had. They kept saying how much they loved each other and that maybe it was time to give their son a sibling.

Without them realizing I came up behind them and slit her husbands throat. I could feel the warm blood squirting out tripping down my hand. He dropped and died almost instantly. Before she could scream I covered her mouth, that mouth that I dreamt about kissing so many nights.

She bit my hand and so I struck her on the head causing her to faint. I ripped off her dress and made her mine in the most brutal way. I became a madman, at last, she was mine! All mine! I had waited for this moment so long. I panted as of possessed, afterwards I plunged the knife into her chest repeatedly and then fled.

As soon as I got home I showered and burned the clothes I was wearing. That was the only night I could sleep.

The following day, the whole town found out about what happened to the couple.

People couldn't stop questioning who could be capable of committing such a horrible crime. I was scared that somebody might find out it was me so I moved to a different city. I came back about three months ago and now almost no one talks about them.
No one ever found out it was me who killed that couple."

"What was her name?" I asked fearing what the answer would be.

Celeste. Celeste Alvarado.

The tears stream down my face. My cheeks burned with anger. I felt enraged, I wanted to scream, I felt impotence. In that moment I wished I wasn't a priest so I could just beat this man.

Why did I have to hear this confession?

My Lord, why did my grandparents hide the truth from me?

They told me my parents had been killed in an assault, but never that my mom had been raped.

My mother, whose name was Celeste Alvarado!

"Father, please, help me, I need to be forgiven. I need to know God has forgiven me so I can go on with my life, Father…are you listening to me?"

During my studies at the seminary I was never prepared to hear a confession like this…

How can I give this man absolution?

HOW CAN I ABSOLVE THE MURDERER OF MY PARENTS?

CYBER CONNECTION

I was so caught up in my thoughts and I barely noticed a confession time was almost over. I was hoping that no one else would show so I could go to the chapel a long while. I was in need of comfort, the comfort that only prayer can give you. I hear the rustic small window of the confessional room open and then a deep voice say, "father I have send gravely." It didn't belong to anyone from the town.

"Hail Mary full of Grace" I said

After almost of minute of silence I tried to push him to talk.

"Go ahead my son, tell me your sins. Our Lord loves greatly and his mercy is infinite. Have no fear, you talking to one of his servants. I am an instrument of the Lord to help you find the peace you seek"

"Father…" He says with a broken voice I can so he was crying, "I'm a killer."

I freeze when I hear the words.

I had never heard someone say those words in my entire life as a priest, but I knew that I needed to listen to him.

"You see father, I came to this town looking for a guy"

"What for?" I ask

"I'll start from the beginning...

I met Raul through a chat for a gay man, well at least he told me that was his name. I thought he was the most handsome man that I had seen in a long time. At first he seemed very timid, he spoke very little about his private life but always asked me questions about sex. I could tell he was simply curious and maybe had no close friends to discuss these things with.

Shortly after becoming virtual friends we spoke openly about sex with no boundaries. I was taken by surprise at the way he expressed himself he spoke like an adult when in reality he was still a teenager.

Approximately two months after chatting. I asked him for his email address suggesting we could communicate through there also. By then I had his complete trust, soon after he gave me his phone number and I called him almost every night he started to tell me about his parents and siblings.

I knew he felt lonely having to keep quiet his sexual preferences and I realized that he was into older man like me maybe even older. Which made me happy because at 55 years old and having failed in two serious relationships it was becoming difficult to find someone who was interested in me. I had all of his attention which made me become obsessed with him.

As our bond got deeper and I conversations more intense I build the courage to ask him to send me a nude photo.

I expected him to get upset but I was surprised when he accepted. He sent me not only one but at least a dozen photos of himself. In all the photos he was smiling exposing his naked body. He asked me to do the same thing, but instead of sending him photos of myself I sent him naked photos of other men which I took from the Internet. For some reason I believed that the day we had to meet in person he wouldn't realize the difference.

Or virtual relationship continued like this for about six months. It consisted of phone calls, emails, chats via WebCam. A strange mixture of feelings begin to emerge. For example, if he'd call me and I couldn't speak because I was working he'd become upset and accuse me of being with other men. If I wanted to talk to him and he was unable to I'd immediately become full of jealousy thinking that he was with someone else, although I knew that he wasn't allowed to go out into town by himself. When I was down, hearing his laugh was enough to help me feel better. If he was depressed I'd sing to him over the phone and tell him that I loved him and I could immediately hear a change in his tone.

Everything was great, until the day that I told him I wanted to meet him in person. He thought I was joking, but gave me the address to his house anyway. I really did want to meet him though.

When I told him that I had my vacation dates set and money saved up for the trip he asked me to not go through with it. To please not even think about going to find him, no one in his family knew what he was doing and in reality he thought he was just confused sexually. He said he felt attracted to both men and women.

I became enraged, I felt as if he had just played with me. Instead of trying to comprehend him I said something he shouldn't have:

"I'm going to go find you, and not only that, I'm going to print out our conversations and your photos. I'm going to show them to everyone. All your family and friends will know who you really are."

He begged me for forgiveness, said that he never intended to hurt me. That if I followed through with my threat his father would kill him being as he's a homophobic, to please just forget about him.

I told him there was no changing my mind that I would see him face-to-face in a few days. That he needed to prepare himself for our inevitable encounter instead.

The next day, once I had calm down. I thought better about everything. I realized I was being unfair with him and that I couldn't do what I said I would. He was just a young boy who needed help so I canceled my flight.

I sent him a message five days ago letting him know that I would no longer reach out to him. I advised him to seek professional help and to try to better his relationship with his parents, I told him to ask for help at school or with his friends but he never answered.

I sent him various text messages to asking him to please check his email, with no response. I began to worry since he didn't answer, so I came looking for him, I only wanted to see him briefly, to know he was alright. I wanted to apologize for hurting him and saying the things I did, I wanted to let him know that I was going to step out of his life and I wished him nothing but the best.

I got into town last night and I stayed at the only hotel I could find. I went to a bar and that's when I heard the news.

His name wasn't Raul it was Rodrigo...and he'd committed suicide.

One of the patrons at the bar showed me the newspaper. I recognized him in the photo, that's how I found out what his real name was.

It was a terrible blow for me. I swear, father. I didn't want to cause him any harm, that's why came to look for him, his silence concerned me. We used to talk every day, at all hours.

His death wounded me deeply! I feel as if I had been the one who killed him.

Father help me. What can I do so his parents forgive me without tainting the memory they have of Rodrigo?"

I am dumbfounded.

"I want to know your name" I say to the man.

"Well for, father? Are you going to take me to the authorities?"

"You know I can't do that, the seal of confession is inviolable. I just want to know the name of the man who is responsible and indirectly for causing one family so much pain, one who had to find the body of a Rodrigo hanging in his room, without a single note explaining why. The man responsible for the pain that the mother is suffering right now at lost of her youngest son. The man responsible for the desperation that the father felt not been able to do anything to revive his son. The man responsible indirectly for the tears wept and the pain felt by my mom as she buried her grandchild."

RODRIGO WAS MY NEPHEW!

SENTENCED TO DEATH

I am a priest and I'm beginning to feel resentment. I am a priest and suddenly I have the urge to hit him, hurt him, make him pay.

I am a priest and I feel I can relate to the words Jesus spoke,

"My God, my God. Why have you forsaken me?"

"Have you told anyone?"

I knew who it was as soon as I heard the voice, full with ironing, I'll never forget it. Not as long as I lived.

I was waiting for a confession time to be over so I could go rest. For a while I had been feeling terribly tired and I couldn't understand why I was still very young.

"Mario, are you going to answer me?"

When he said my name, it sounded as if he were mocking me, so cynical.

"Why have you come?" I tried to sound as calm as possible, but it's impossible. I know he can hear my voice shaking, I'm almost sure he can hear my heart racing. He knows very well that his presence terrorizes me.

"I've come to confess myself and…"

"Don't mock me Eduardo" I interrupt him, "Don't forget that this is the house of God, and although you can do with the world what you wish, lie to people, you can't lie to God."

"Oh, Eduardo?...I see you haven't forgotten my name"

Forget his name? As if it were that easy to forget the name of someone who cause so much pain. Who harmed me so much. As if a simple apology could make everything go away. I will definitely never forget his name, his face, or what he has done to me.

As hard as I try, I cannot forget what happened a few months back...

I had just arrived to the village where I was assigned priest to a parish. Everyone welcomed me with arms wide open. Through conversations I had with my parishioners, I learned about the people. That's how I learned about Eduardo.

Eduardo, he was the typical macho male. Since he was the son of the mayor and had a lot of money, he believed he could to whatever he pleased. He abused his power, spent most of his time at bars consuming alcohol without paying, and his nights with different women.

Margarita, one of the best catechist the parish had who also happens to be the prettiest girl in town, mentioned to me that Eduardo was pursuing her and told her that he wanted to marry her. She felt that she was in love with him, and believed the love he claimed to have for her to be sincere.

I warned her to be cautious with him. To not be so quick to believe his word, to pay attention to his actions this would show her if he was truly in love with her or was just playing with her emotions like he did with many women.

Margarita mentioned our conversation to Eduardo. He began to harass me, felt I was against him, in reality all I wanted was for Margarita to not suffer.

One night, a man came knocking on the parish door. He claimed that there was a gravely wounded man at the gate. He said this man asked him to please come find me so he could confess his sins and die in peace. Without hesitation I grabbed my stole and holy oils and a jacket because it was cold. I followed the man to where he said the wounded man was lying. Once there I didn't see anyone and then I heard Eduardo's voice, "You are too naïve, father. I thought it'd be a bit more challenging to get you out of your home. It's time for you to see what I'm capable of, you should've never messed with me!"

I felt a hard blow to my head when I tried turning around. I lost consciousness, without a doubt that was a blessing, so I wouldn't feel the atrocities Eduardo would inflict upon me.

I woke up a few hours later, my body have been be in. I bled from many places, I was hurting everywhere, I felt a pain that made me realize what the worst act done to me was.

I was able to stand up. In pain, scared, and full of shame I hurried to the parish. I got into the shower, ran the cold water to ease the pain, I wished with all my heart that the water would not only help me get rid of the dirt and blood but that it would also wash away the pain and humiliation I felt.

The following day, after a sleepless nights, I call for the village sexton, Don Felipe. I asked him to post a sign outside the door announcing that mass would be canceled because the priest had been mugged and beaten the night before and therefore was unable to complete his tasks. The news flew.

Margarita and the rest of the catechists helped keep the house clean and tended to my wounds. I never spoke about what happened. I couldn't bring myself to do it, and I was sure it wouldn't happen again.

"…so chances are, you also have it. So Mario, what're you going to do?"

I was so consumed in my thoughts that I didn't realize he was talking to me.

"What did he say? Repeat what you just told me."

"Oh Mario, Mario, Mario, Mario" he says mockingly, "I see you like to suffer well I'll tell you once again. But I'll cut to the chase. A few weeks ago I started to feel sick and since I've been with so many women from the bar I went to the doctor to get checked out. They informed me two days ago that I tested positive for aids. I've only got a few months to live due to how advanced the virus is. Anyway, remember what happened that night? Remember what I did to you? Chances are you have it too."

I was flabbergasted!! My God this can't be!!

"So Mario…tell me. What are you gonna do?
HOW ARE YOU GOING TO TELL YOUR FAMILY AND COMMUNITY THA YOU HAVE AIDS?

Deep within me, I feel the words that Jesus spoke as he was being nailed to the cross…

"MY GOD, MY GOD. WHY HAVE YOU FORSAKEN ME?"

THE CANDYMAN

From the moment I saw him walk into the temple, I knew something was wrong. It wasn't common for him to come around.

If I remember correctly it had been more than five years since I saw him around here. As a matter of fact, since I was assigned pastor in my hometown I only saw him a handful of times. In the beginning I insisted over in over that he come to church, He always denied, saying that he didn't believe in anything or anyone. Many people asked why he didn't come around for mass as well, it was a very difficult time. After sometime though, we all got used to him not being around. So seeing him here all of a sudden worried me.

I was putting up an image of the Virgin Mary that a family donated to the parish. When I heard the footsteps behind me and turned around to see him.

"I must speak with you, but in secrecy of confession" he said.

In secret of confession? Things must be worse than I supposed. It had been years since he confessed himself. I went for my still and invited him to the confessional room. He declined my invitation saying, "Please Henry, we know each other too well for any of that. I prefer the sacristy."

We enter the sacristy and I put two chairs facing one another. Assuming that he did not want to kneel, I knew him to well.

Once we were face-to-face Stephen began to speak...

"You've known since young kids I have always been clever and ambitious. I've always contemplated of ways to make a fortune. A fortune I finally have, but one that I am at risk of losing if you do not help me.

I know the police have been following my footsteps for a few days now. Because someone snitched and said that my candies are specially prepared."

"Specially prepared? I don't understand Stephen"

"My candies, the ones I sell in the next town, they contain drugs."

"You're selling drugs?" I interrupt, "My God, I can't believe it! Now I understand why you can live the lifestyle you do."

"Come on Henry, don't tell me that you didn't at least suspect something? I've been doing it for quite some time now. Selling it to the elementary school kids and the middle school kids. I've never sold them here because someone can easily recognize me. There it's easier to go unnoticed. But someone said something, probably the competition. The cops have been looking into me for days now. That's not my biggest problem though, I'm very cautious to only have the money when I know the kids have money to buy. I use a hat, I put on a fake mustache, and always wear sunglasses."

"So then what's the problem?"

"Well about three weeks ago or so, one of the boys I sell to in the middle school, Elias, began to ask me for candy in bigger quantities. He said it was so he could give his friends, obviously this was good for me because my sales go up. In reality he was just becoming more addicted.

This morning I sold him two dozen. A boy saw the deal go down, but I wasn't too worried because he's never seen me before and like I said, I'm always disguised. Well this afternoon I drove by the school again to see if Elias wanted to buy some more candy, sometimes he does. I saw him behind the bathrooms, that's when I saw him eat all the candies at once. I was the only one to see him. A few moments later he began convulsing, The same boy that saw our deal go down earlier approached him when he saw what was happening. Once he saw that he couldn't do anything for him he ran for help. That's when I jumped the gate to see if he had any more candy around him. When I saw that there was nothing that could incriminate me I left. But I've heard about this occurring before with others, by now he's probably dead. He only thing that could incriminate me now, is that boy who saw our deal occur this morning."

I feel a chill down my spine.

"So, after talking to you I'm going home to spend the rest of the day with mom. I'm pretty sure they're going to question me. I'm going to tell them I was with you.

Obviously they're going to come a question you next, and you going to tell him the truth, that I was confessing myself with you. I'm denying that I was ever at the school. They won't doubt what you say since you're a pastor and all."

"How can you ask me for such a thing? Why are you trying to make me your accomplice?"

"Technically you wouldn't be lying. I've been here for sometime now I was sitting outside the church for a little bit. I wouldn't be lying when I tell them that I've been here for hours. Besides you know that mom already had one heart attack, and the doctor said her body wouldn't be able to sustain another one. Think about her, could you live with yourself if she were to die from a second one. Knowing you could've prevented it?...answer me, Henry."

"ARE YOU GOING TO HELP OR CONDEMN YOUR ONLY BROTHER?"

THE PEDOPHILE

I had just reached the parsonage when my cell phone rings. I was tired, I had been working with the youth group since 9 in the morning and it was already 5 in the afternoon. We were building a house with several workshops. We'd be offering computer, electronic, tailoring, and carpentry classes, all free of charge. The land we were building it on was donated by the city. Our mission was to have a place where young people could learn stuff for free, keeping them away from bad habits. At 7 I had mass, then confessions for an hour, then dinner, after that prayer time, then I went to bed. Every day I woke up at 5 AM.

The phone call was from the hospital, informing me that a man had been run over and that he was in critical condition. He was asking to confess himself. I needed to hurry, so I grab my stole, prayer book, and holy oils. I take a taxi to get there quicker.

Since I was assigned to be pastor of this parish three years ago, I have served the community as much as I can. I told the hospital to call me whenever they required my services no matter what time it was. I celebrate a mass in their chapel every week, for the sick and their family. We also have people from the parish who go during the week to pray with the sick and take them communion.

As soon as they arrive to the hospital, Lupita, one of the nurses rushes to me, "Father Daniel please hurry the man they got hit is in critical condition, and he won't stop asking for a priest."

She guides me to the room. And once there gives us privacy. I get close to him, he looks about 50 years old. His face was swollen from the injuries he sustained. He could hardly open his eyes and I could hardly hear his voice, "Father, I'm going to die I know it…"

"Relax my child, don't strain yourself too much, as long as you repent from the bottom of your heart all your sins, you will be okay."

"No father, I need you to listen to me. I can't die without confessing my sins."

"Hail Mary full of Grace" I say

"Conceived without sin" he responds

"Okay son, I'm listening to you. Tell me, what are your sins?" I say taking his hand.

"For many years I've carried a burden because of a sin I committed. I haven't been able to live in peace and I need to know that God is forgiving me for it. Many years ago, when I was a newlywed. A couple moved across from us. A couple with a young child. Both of them worked, and my wife offered to babysit the child who was six. He was a calm child, not mischievous at all and very obedient. My wife was really delighted with him, she said it was nice to have him keep her company and it helped her get practice for when she became a mother.

Everything was fine, until one afternoon as I got home from work the neighbor came to our door. He said his wife was very sick and he had to take her to the hospital. He asked us to watch his son for a few more hours, and my wife said yes. Wow my wife made dinner, I played with the little boy. He was really fascinating, he did everything we asked, he was very trusting.

We were jumping around the living room when he fell and hit his knee. Without hesitation I pick him up and sitting on my lap.

"Don't cry I'll rub it and it won't hurt anymore" I say to him.

"With the pain go away soon?" He asked

"Yes it will, especially because I'm going to rub it with a lot of care."

"Thank you" he said as he hugged me around the neck.

As I caressed his leg, I felt something strange. Something inside me really enjoyed having him on my lap, at the same time it scared me. Something inside me told me to stop, but I disregarded the thought. I continue to caress the little boys leg, then I stuck my hand up his shorts, when he felt this he turned up and looked at me with a very innocent eyes.

"Don't be scared, if you hold still the pain will soon go away. You can't tell anyone though, because then everyone is going to want me to rub their legs when they get hurt. You promise to keep our secret?"

"Okay, I won't say anything to anyone."

I kept my hand inside his shorts for quite some time caressing him, until I heard my wife calling us to go have dinner.

We ate in silence. Each time I glanced to look at the little boy he looked down. Once we finished eating dinner I told my wife that I would go for a walk with the boy, that this would help him digest his food anyway. I grab his hand and we go outside.

"What did you feel when I put my hand inside your shorts?"

"I don't know, but it scared me."

"Don't be scared, it made the pain go away, but remember it has to be our secret, okay?"

"Okay"

As I'm walking back into the house. I hear my wife anxiously talking on the phone. She sounds like she's about to cry.

"Honey, my mom got very sick, I need to go spend the night with her. Can you please watch the child until his dad gets home?"

"Don't worry honey, I'll take care of him."

About a half hour after my wife leaves the house the phone rings. It was our neighbor.
"I'm sorry to be taking advantage of you, but my wife got worse. The doctors are suggesting I stay here in case of an emergency. Would you mind of my son spends the night at your house?"

"Don't worry about your son, we will take care of him. I hope your wife gets well soon"

"Thank you so much. You have no idea how grateful I am."

Father I don't want to going to details but, after I told him he would be spending the night; I had him sleep in my bed and I raped him. I told him that it was normal and that everyone did it. I asked that he never speak of it with anyone. I told him I would always care for him. The following day his mother died, his dad was devastated and they moved away. I never heard anything about them again."

His voice started breaking,

"Father, do you think God could forgive me? I feel the need to see him, to ask for his forgiveness. To tell him that I suffered very much once his dad took him away. I wanted to explain to him what I did, what had been done to me. I wanted him to understand that this is a like a chain…"

"I'm sure God has forgiven you" I say with tears in my eyes, "you can leave in peace and be in his presence, I assure you that not everyone has to continue this cycle you speak of. Some chains should be broken, and that little boy broke free from that chain. After his mother died his dad took him to live with his grandparents. He had therapy sessions with a very good psychologist, this is how he was able to understand what happened to him. He had been victim of a pedophile. That although that man may have touched his body, he never touched his soul or heart. He learned to overcome and forgive. Now he is a man who can tell you from the bottom of his heart that you are forgiven.

THAT MAN IS ME!!!"

CONCEIVED WITHOUT SIN

While at the seminary, very few times I asked myself what my first confession would be like. When I did think about it, I imagined my first time hearing someone's confessions, to probably be with one of those older women that are always at church and who participate in any church activity. Or maybe it'd be a child, confessing their sins for the first time in order to do his first communion.

That they arrived of my retaining as a priest. I was assigned to the parish, The Divine Face. The head pastor, Father Ruben Jaramillo, told me I could be his nephew since we had the same last name, only that I'd be adopted.

He was my mentor. He spoke to me about listening to people's sins. Told me what the most common sins were, he said I needed to listen with patience when people spoke. If I felt like they were holding back to encourage them to open up. I needed to be prudent, but more importantly make sure that they knew that no matter what their faults were; God loved them. I needed to help them understand that God loves the sinner but not the sin.

I was nervous when the day finally came in which I had to hear confessions. I went into the temple to pray for a bit, to ask God to illuminate me, to send me his Holy Spirit so I'd be able to listen and guide these people who were repenting. After I was a little more calm I walk into the confessional room kiss my stool and waited for the first penitent.

I expected to hear all sorts of things, but I was not prepared to hear this. This was simply an aberration!

My God. Just how far will a man go for power?

How badly will ambition blind a man?

"Hail Mary full of Grace"

"Conceived without sin" it was a man.

"When was the last time you've confessed child?

"Quite frankly, I'm not sure. I don't think I've done it since I was a teenager"

"Why?"

"I only believes in God up until my teen years. When I went away for college it was difficult to keep my faith. I stopped believing in him. I also became very egotistical once I completed my career. I was the top of my class. Finally, because I was waiting for the opportunity to confess my sins with you."

"What do you mean, I don't understand your last reason?"

"Exactly what I said. I was waiting for the opportunity to confess my sins with you."

"Tell me son, what are your sins" I wasn't sure what to say in response to what I had just heard, "God will forgive you if he sees that you have a repentant heart.

"I do feel terrible for what I did. But I would do it again, because it was all worth it."

I mummur, "I don't understand, a sin that you repent about but you say was worth committing?"

"I will be as brief, clear and explicit as possible. I know there's other people waiting to confessor sins. And I don't want to abuse by taking up too much of your time. Aside from that, there's some things that I might need to further explain in order to get you to completely understand. So I will try to sum up everything in as few words as possible.

Since high school all my teachers told me I was very smart. That regardless of the career that I decided to pursue, they believe I'd get far. I decided to pursue a career in medicine. I graduated with honors and soon after the offers came in from hospitals all over the place.

I chose a hospital strictly for women. It was locates in downtown. I was very intrigued by how the woman's body worked. I found it fascinating they had the capability of giving life but that there were some that couldn't procreate.

I alternated my time between curing diseases and conducting secrets studies. I was very cautious to not get caught because not only could I lose my job but also my license to practice. In 1978 the world learned that in England the first girl was born out of an artificially inseminated egg, then another in Spain in 1984. I was proud, because although the world didn't knower, I was responsible for the first child who was born from a artificially inseminated egg. I was the father to that baby, the first baby born from an artificially inseminated egg that would not go down known in history. I decided to keep quiet about the whole thing being as everything didn't go as planned.

In 1976 I already knew what needed to be done. I just need to find a woman who is willing to undergo the experiment. It wasn't an easy task, since little information was known about the matter there was no one jumping at the opportunity to do it. A lot of complications could also occur if fertilization was established. So I decided that I would perform the procedure on a woman without her knowing it.

One day, a very religious and beautiful young lady came to the hospital. She was accompanied by an older woman, the mother superior. The young girl was novice who had just made her vows to God. She only required a simple surgery on her appendix, I decided she was the one. I performed the procedure on her without her knowing and fertilized her egg.

The baby that came from the fertilization had been conceived without sin.

I told her that she needed to return for a few visits to ensure that there had not been any complications with her surgery. This was my excuse so I could keep a close eye on her. All of a sudden she stopped showing up for her visits. I learned she was expelled from the convents after discovering her pregnancy. I did my research, and found out where she lived. The poor woman was alone, housed in a shelter. Her family disowned her after finding out about the baby she was expecting. Throughout her entire pregnancy I made sure she had money. I asked two friends of mine who were married to help me get the money to her. I told them that I just felt bad for her and wanted to help her during difficult time. They never questioned me. She gave birth to a strong boy, but unfortunately died after. Knowing that my friends had very kind hearts I asked them to adopt a child. They gladly did being as they couldn't have babies of their own. I even suggested that they name him Emmanuel.

The death of the woman took it's toll on me. I never imagined that these would be the consequences to my actions. I promise to never let my ego get the best of me again."

I sat there in silence, waiting to see if there was something else a man wanted to add.

After a moment I asked, "Why was I chosen to hear your confession?"

"Because I have stomach cancer and have a very short time to live. I guess in the end it's didn't help me much to be so excellent with medicine, being as I can't help myself. I tried to chemotherapy, but the cancer just won't go away. I also decided to confess sins to you because I am the biological father to that baby born through artificial insemination. That baby who has grown up to be a priest."

"What are you trying to say?" I ask in the halting voice

"Those friends of mine who I asked to please adopt the child are Antonio Jaramillo and Gloria Santana."

MY GOODNESS! MY NAME IS EMMANUEL. MY PARENTS ARE ANTONIO AND GLORIA!!

MATRICIDE

The phone rang incessantly. I looked at the clock on my nightstand table, it was 2:30 AM. At first I confused the ringing with my house phone. Once I pressed the answer button and the ringing continued, I realized that it was my cell phone ringing and not my house phone. My parishioners called my house phone when there was an emergency at the parish, but only my family called myself phone.

"Hello" I say

"May please speak with Father Navarro please" the man on the other end says

"Speaking, may I ask who's calling?" I ask

"I'm officer Ryan Terranova, it is urgent that you come to your parents' home. Something tragic has occurred but I can't give the details over the phone. Please hurry we're waiting" he responds.

As soon as I hang up with the cop. I get up and get dressed. It's cold outside. I only let the car warm up a bit and I rush off to my parents' home.

The drive there felt eternal. My parents lived 35 minutes away from the city where I was a pastor. I'm sure I made it to their home in record time that night though. I enjoyed going to visit them on my days off. We usually go out and eat somewhere, or spend the day outdoors, sometimes we'd simply stay in and play board games.

When he finally arrived to the home, I saw a lot of patrol vehicles, an ambulance, some neighbors, and even a reporter or two. I quickly park and run towards the house to see what's going on. Once the people see, they quickly move aside to clear the path for me. I walk into the house and see something the blows me away...

My brother Alan, 20 years old, was sitting on the sofa, handcuffed. He was wearing only boxer briefs and had scratches and traces of blood on different parts of his body. His gaze seemed lost, his eyes were dilated. There was two cops with him, one of them looks at me and says:

I'm Ryan Terranova, are you Father Philip?"

"Yes" I reply

After my brother heard my voice he turned towards me and said, "It's all your fault!"

I wasn't sure what to say or do. The policemen turned to look at my brother and then at me again. Ryan asks:

"Why is he saying that you're to blame?"

"I'm not sure sir, may speak to him alone?" I ask

"I'm afraid that's not possible Ryan said. He just committed a crime and we have to take him down to the station. Besides he seems to be under the influence of some sort of drug and it is evident that he has been consuming a lot of alcohol. He's refusing to say anything, so he's coming with us. We were just awaiting your arrival, to see if you could identify the bodies. We called you because we found your number in the phonebook on top of the table."

I see the phonebook that Ryan is talking about. It's opened to a page exposing my name and cell number.

My voice is shaking, "Wait a second sir, did you just say bodies?"

"Yes, please follow me."

Ryan escorts me to my parents' room. The scene couldn't to be more painful and bloody.

My dad's body is face down on the floor. He was wearing the pajamas I gave them last Father's Day. He has multiple stab wounds on his back. I see my mother's body on her bed, she's covered with a sheet. As I get closer I see that she is naked. What was the meaning of this?

Ryan and I walk back to the living room. When my brother sees us, he starts repeating the same thing, "It's your fault!"

The other cop asks, "Talk to him maybe in this state of mind he'll tell you why he's blaming you."

I sit next to my brother. I put my hand on his shoulder and he reacts as if he had been struck by lightning, "Don't touch me! Everything is your fault!"

"Alan, please look at me. It's me, Philip, your brother. Can you tell me what happened?"

"I didn't want to do it. But she never love me the way she loved you. Ever since I was a kid, all I heard her talk about, was how proud she was of you, for being a top student in school. Then you went away to the seminary. I thought that I'd finally have her all to myself, but of course that only made her more proud of you. She said it was a privilege to be the mother of a priest.

I loved her, but she never understood that. For me there was no other woman more beautiful than her. I tried looking for that love in other women, but that was all in vain, no woman could compare to her…"

"Alan! She was her mother. How could you look at her that way? Besides she loves us both equally" I say interrupting him.

"Lies! She only loved you. I never felt a bit of love like the one she showed for you."

Not able to hold back the tears anymore I ask, "is that why you did it?"

There wasn't any doubt that it was him who had killed our parents.

"I didn't want to kill her! I didn't want to kill her! When I got home from the bar, she came out to open a door for me because I lost my keys. She had never look as beautiful as she did tonight. I told her that and I tried kissing her when she slapped me. She went to her room and I followed. I tried telling her how much I loved her, and she slapped me again. I lost all self-control and I made her mine. She was screaming when dad got home. He came in with a kitchen knife and we started to fight, I couldn't hold back."

"Stop it! Please! I don't want to hear anymore! Gentlemen, please take him, I think he's going to need to see a psychiatrist."

A reporter walks in. I'm not sure how she was able to convince comps to let her in. She immediately turns on her recorder and asks:

"FATHER PHILIP! IS IT TRUE THAT YOUR VERY OWN BROTHER RAPED AND KILLED HER ALONG WITH YOUR FATHER?

IN BETWEEN DUTY AND LIFE

Ramon Chavez Contreras. Where had I heard the name before? Ramon Chavez Contreras. I couldn't quite put my finger on it but I was sure I knew from somewhere.

It had been a few minutes since I landed in the St. Louis Missouri airport, when I saw Father Dylan Schrader. He was the priest in Jefferson City, and I mentioned to him that I'd be in town for a few days. My parents were amongst his parishioners. I would've loved to stay with my parents' in their home, but Father Dylan said that he was in need of Latin priests. He asked me to stay with him, so I could assist in planning some events for the community, he thought this might help attract more people being as they'd feel more comfortable with someone who spoke their language.

The drive from St. Louis to Jefferson City is a bit long. Almost a 2 hour drive. The drive went by rather fast though, Father Dylan and I had plenty to converse about. The English classes I had taken were really helping me. I took advantage of any opportunity I had to practice my English, especially when I traveled to the United States.

"Ramon Chavez Contreras, that's the men who is being held in Bowling Green. He's been a prisoner for almost a year and tomorrow is his execution. It's such a shame that when he was arrested there was no one around who spoke Spanish. He was in great need of a Latin lawyer, sadly there aren't any around here. I thought maybe you could go see him, so he could confess his sins. He must be desperate not being able to do so since he speaks very little English."

"Ramon Chavez Contreras, I'm sure I know that name from somewhere. Father, if you don't mind if like to go see him today." I say

"Don't you want to get some rest and see your parents first?" he asks.

"I can visit them later or tomorrow. Something tells me I must go see this man at once."

Once in Jefferson City, I get off the car simply to take down my luggage. Then we head to Bowling Green to see Ramon. I was sure that once I saw his face, everything would dawn on me. We were on the road for another two hours.

When we got to the prison we left most of my possessions in the car. I went to the town were our IDs.

A guard greeted us and asked us for our IDs. We handed them to him, he inspected them under a UV lights, to verify that they were authentic. Since I told him that I was there because Ramon wanted to confess his sins I was taken to a special room where I could speak to him face-to-face and privately. All the other visitors had to visit their loved ones in a room in which they had to communicate using telephones with a thick glass separating the prisoners from their family.

The room I was escorted to was completely empty. I took a seat in a few moments later Ramon showed up.

He was about 5'7, he was wearing the traditional orange overalls prisoners are required to wear. His untidy curly hair fell over his forehead. He walked upright and it was obvious he'd work out while in prison. He had light brown eyes, but he didn't seem sad or upset. I was taken back by this, I asked myself how someone who knew he only had a few hours left to live could be so calm.

"Good afternoon Father" he says giving me a firm hand shake, "I couldn't believe it when I was told I had a visitor. You were the first person to come see me, you have no idea how thankful I am."

"Good afternoon Ramon, I just arrived from Mexico and father Dylan, the pastor from Jefferson City told me about you. He told me about your situation and I wanted to come see if you wanted to confess yourself."

"A confession? Father, you see, I'm at piece with myself. I would like to, however, tell you how everything happened. The reason why I spending my last moments of life here."

"So you're not interested in a confession?" I say as I prepare to put my stole away.

"You know what, yes, I want this to be in secrecy of confession. Anyway, there's nothing anyone can do to help me anymore at this point."

I take my stole and kiss it. I put it over my shoulders and wait for Ramon to begin with his confession.

"Everything happened about a year ago. I had only been in Jefferson City for about six months and I hadn't quite adjusted to the lifestyle change. I really wanted to work, save up a good amount of money and settle down in Mexico.
I didn't have enough money to pay the man who i was recommended to, to help me cross the border. I reached out to

my best friend who lives in Jefferson City, he offered to lend me the money I needed so I'd be able to make the trip.

It's not easy crossing the border illegally. I had to walk for almost 30 hours, but I was extremely thankful to God for allowing me to make it on my first try. I've heard stories of many people who have to try multiple times, stories of others that get deported back after they get caught by border patrol, and some of people who have died trying, so I felt extremely grateful.

My friend told me I could stay in his home. He lived with his sister and his parents. His house has three bedrooms so he and I would share one.

I began to work at a Mexican restaurant as a dishwasher. The job was tough but I felt extremely blessed. I had a job and my friend's family was really good to me. I couldn't ask for anything more the time.

After some time, I realized that my friend was heading down the wrong path. I caught him a few times with jewelry and expensive watches which kept hidden underneath his bed. I heard rumors that he was selling and consuming drugs. It was tough for me to learn this, because Abel was more than a friend to me, he was like a brother."

"Abel? Your buddy's name is Abel?" I ask

"Yes…One evening, after his parents had gone to bed. I asked if we could go for a walk in the park. I told him I wanted to discuss something very serious with him. He said yes, but asked that I head out first because he had something to do. He said he had to meet up with a friend so he asked that I wait for him buy some from pools in the park. I waited for him for almost an hour, it was almost midnight. I started to think that he wasn't going to show when suddenly I saw him running towards me…

"Ramon, you have to help me."

"What is it?" I see blood on his shirt

"I got into a bit of an argument with some guy, I met him at the other park. We started fighting and when I saw that he had a pocketknife I pulled out mine and I killed him! Please Ramon, I need to take responsibility. I can't let my mom find out what I did. She has a heart condition, and before you came to the US she had a heart attack. That's doctor said she wouldn't survive a second one. I promise to find the best lawyer to get you out of jail as soon as possible. Please, I've never asked you for anything and I know this is a lot to ask but don't do it for me, do it for my mother. Please?"

I told him I would take the blame. I felt indebted to him. After all, he'd been the one who lent me the money so I could come here. His parents welcomed me with arms wide open, and I didn't want anything to happen to his mom, Ms. Teresa. She treated me as if I were her own son, and if I could protect her from such grief, I'd gladly do it. Besides Abel promised to find me a good lawyer."

I tried to say something but Ramon didn't allow me to.

"Please, allow me to continue. I went to turn myself into the authorities. Abel told me where to find the body. I took the police there and show them the pocketknife that was used to kill him. I even went to the extreme of injuring myself, to make everything more believable. Look I still have the scar."

He shows me the scar on his upper abdomen.

The trial was quick. Since Abel promised to help me, I declared myself guilty of the crime. During the entire trial I never saw him or his parents. I actually haven't seen or heard from them since that night.

After a while I got tired of waiting and realized that he had abandoned me.

I don't resent Abel, father. You know why? Because he helped me in my time of need. His parents treated me well. If he felt this is how I needed to repay him for his help, then so be it. I'll die in peace, there's is no room for negative feelings in my heart...why are you crying, father?"

"Because you are a man full of kindness. You could've easily declined yourself to helping him, but you didn't. You sacrificed yourself to keep a mother from hurting the way she would've had she seen her arrested and and convicted for a crime he committed. Mostly though, because you were a victim of of a lie and great injustice.

I regret hearing your story in secrecy of confession. As a priest I am obligated to keep all this secret. I feel so helpless not being able to speak up and get you help."

My God. I think to myself. Ramon is going to die unjustly.

My younger brother's name is Abel. I now remember, how he always spoke of his best friend, Ramon Chavez Contreras. He lied to Ramon, my mom doesn't suffer from any heart disease. She's always been very strong and healthy.

How can I save Ramon's life? I can't speak of this confession.

MY GOD! What can I do for Ramon?

THE SURPRISE

I was determined to find her. She was usually very punctual on Fridays to gather the food everyone made to then give out at hospitals. As a matter of fact, she was the one who came up with the whole thing: "Action and Movement"

The weekly meeting started at 2:00 PM on the dot. All the women arrived prepared to cook. They had 2 hours to get all the dishes ready. After we'd split in groups and go to different hospitals to donate the food and talk to the family of the sick. She always said, "People in hospitals don't only need to fed food, but also words that will alleviate them, encourage them."

Around 6 PM all the woman gathered at the parish for about 15 minutes, then went home. Today she didn't show, everyone found it strange being as she never missed a meeting. I called her cell, but got no answer. I decided I'd go to her home after my confession hour was up. Besides, we agreed that tonight I'd go to her home so together we could give her husband the surprise.

I look down at my watch. It's 8:00 PM, I still have one hour remaining. I peek out of the confessional room to see if anyone was waiting to repent, I decided that if no one was in sight of leave early to find her. I had a strange feeling in my chest. As soon as I poke my head out I see him walking in.

"Good evening father Robert. Let me guess, you're wondering why I'm here and why Samantha didn't show up for the weekly reunion…can we talk in secrecy of confession? I see there's still time to do so."

I perceived an ironic tone in his voice. There was something different in his gaze, you could say there was a spark of evil in his eyes. It was strange to me. In the time that I'd known him and Samantha, he'd always been very well-mannered and polite.

"Good evening Matthew, of course we can. Go ahead, I'm listening."

Once we're settled in. He begins…

"Look father Robert, I'm not going to beat around the bush. I came here to confess this to you, because I want you to feel the same pain I felt when I found out my wife was being unfaithful to me and…"

"Silence, don't you dare speak of Samantha like that. Your wife is a exceptional woman, besides…"

"Exceptional woman? Oh please, don't make me laugh. What exceptional about a woman who betrays her husband? At first I didn't want to believe it…I was hoping it was a figment of my imagination. Any doubt I had vanished when I found the note last week: "Father Robert, I can't wait till next week. Matthew has no idea, he is in for quite the surprise. I'm so happy!"

I had already noted a change in her behavior in the previous days. She was always smiling, singing, constantly in a great mood, she had a different sparkle in her eyes, nothing could being her down. I kept wondering what could be the cause of this sudden change. So I met with my closest friends. We met at our usual bar, where we had some drinks. I told them about my suspicions, they agreed. She was cheating on me!

I asked what I should do. They were my closest friends and the people I when in need of advice.

"Cheat on her also, so when she finds out she can't throw anything in your face" said Pedro

"That's not enough punishment, beat her. So she learns to respect you" says Matias

"Cheating on her and beating her won't make him feel better. He should kick her out so her whole family finds out she's been unfaithful" said Ulysses

"What do you think?" I ask Julio

He looked at each one of us, finishing his cigarette. Took another sip from his beer and said two words, "Kill her" then he left the bar.

I say bye to my friends and head home. I thought about beating Samantha, but decided it wasn't worth it after seeing how happy she was. I laid on my bed instead and began to plan out my vengeance.

I remembered that about a year ago I purchased life insurance policies on both of us. I planned out every detail very carefully. I'm not willing to go to jail for murder. I followed through with my plan this afternoon."

"You didn't hurt her right? You're going to be sorry your whole life if you did!"

"Are you threatening me, father? It's not in your best interest, let me tell you" he says mockingly.

"You're blind Matthew, Samantha is..."

"Let me continue. Yesterday I bought a used car. I cut the hose for the brakes. Afterwards I took a taxi home. I asked Samantha to accompany me to pick up a car I had just purchased for her. I told her it was time she have one of her own. She was delighted with the news. After we picked up the car, I challenged her to a friendly race, to celebrate the fact that she had her own car. At first she reluctant to accept, but I managed to change her mind.

We started our engines and off we went. We pressed the gas, as we came up to a curve. I hit my brakes, and I know she tried to do the same. As expected, hers failed and she crashed. Immediately the car burst into flames, all that was left to do was to call for help and play the role of grieving husband...I plan to move away after I collect the insurance money. No one will suspect anything, if they ask I'll simply say that I can't bear being here where everything reminds me of my dead wife. So tell me Father, how do you feel knowing your lovely Samantha is dead?"

"You're a murder! You've demonstrated that you were never worthy of the Samantha's love. When you truly love someone you trust them, you should've asked her, talked to her. I don't know how you are going to live with yourself, after you hear what I have to say...for months I accompanied Samantha to see my brother who is a doctor. She was undergoing a medical treatment, she never told you because she didn't want to disappoint you in case the treatment didn't work. Everything she did, she did with you in mind. All she wanted was to give you the greatest gift a woman can give her husband. Last week, my brother called her with the great news. She asked that I be present when she gave you the news since I had been by her side throughout everything. She was going to surprise you today after we finished here. She was going to give you pictures of the ultrasound and the first pair of shoes she knitted the baby...

YOU'VE JUST KILLED THE MOTHER OF YOUR CHILD!!!"

INCEST

I never imagined I'd find myself contemplating to break my oath to secrecy of confession. But here I was...

My name is Bruno, I am 27 years old, and I am the eldest of 8. I was ordained as priest two years ago, and for six months been assigned as vicar to father Aurelio in the parish of San Rafael, which is in the city I was born and raised in. The bishop assigned me here with my mother in mind. She has been diagnosed with cancer and has little time left to live. I try and spend as much time as I can with her.

Confessions are held on Thursday and Friday afternoons but if someone would like to repent at any other time all they have to do is ask. Father Aurelio listens to confessions on Fridays and I on Thursdays. The village knows this, so they choose who they want to confess their sins to.

This morning I receive a phone call from Father Aurelio, "Bruno, I am meeting with the bishop at 3. I'm afraid I won't be able to make it in time for confessions. Do you mind doing me a favor and filling in for me?"

"Of course I can, take your time. Tell the bishop I say hello."

I go around town visiting the sick to give them the holy communion. This is something, I enjoy very much. Nothing gives me greater satisfaction than seeing their faces filled with peace after receiving the communion.

I also take it to my mom. This allows me to spend some time with her. We talked till about 4 PM, I must go. I have to get ready for the confessional hours.

"Son, please try and talk to Fabiola. She's been distant. It's not like her" she says

"Don't worry mom, it's just she's in the early stages of adolescence. Her behavior is normal. I'll come and check on her tonight and talk to her anyway."

We're open for confessions between 5:00-7:00 PM. The first hour and a half is calm, only a few people stop by. I had a few kids also. It's almost Christmas, I'm pretty sure parents are asking them to do so before Christmas Eve.

At about 6:30 I hear someone come up to the window, that is covered with fabric for discretion purposes. She's crying.

I mumble, "Hail Mary full of grace."

"Help me father, I want to die."

"What's wrong, child? Talk. God will listen and forgive" I say. I recognized the voice.

"Forgive? He should be the one asking me for forgiveness!"

She continued to cry. I asked her to calm down, cautious to not let her recognize my voice. Of she found out it were me, she'd opt out of confession.

She continued once a bit calmer, "Father, why is it the people who are supposed to love is most also hurt us most? Why did this happen to me?

I should be in school right now. I've been feeling sick for days. My best friend went with me to see a doctor on another town, my family is too well known here. My friend lent me the money to pay the doctor, because aside from being my best friend, she also knows what it's like. I just hope she doesn't end up like me."

"What's happened to you?" I say disguising my voice.

"It happened for the first time when I was 9 years old. My mom left town to visit my grandparents. She was away for a week. I was sleeping when I felt the hand on my face. I awakened frightened, until I saw his face. He lay next to me and said he was there to keep me from getting scared. He hugged me and began to undress me. I was shaking, he told me to hold still, that he wouldn't hurt me. But he hurt me a lot, he covered my mouth so I wouldn't scream and wake up my siblings. He continued for what felt like hours to me. She he was finally done he dressed himself and headed to his room, but not before telling me to not speak of what happened. He said it wasn't anything bad but that some people did not understand that and that if my mom found out she'd become upset with me. I was just an innocent little girl!

He's continued this abused for the past 5 years. I don't want to cause my mom any pain so I've never said anything; but I want him to stop hurting me…"

"Cry, let go of the pain"

The sound of her crying merges with mine. My God. She was just a teenager and she had already suffered more than most adults. I asked myself who was the monster that could do such a thing. She continued…

"My best friend has experienced it as well. Her rapist was a cousin of hers, and he did it only once. We share a deep bond because of what we've both experienced. I didn't trust having anyone else come to the doctor with me, other than her. She suggested I come to you for advice. I don't know what I'm going to do when everyone finds out. I don't want to tell my mom the truth, it will cause her a great amount of pain. Father, I'm desperate, the doctor said I'm 3 months pregnant…I'm having a child with my own father!"

"Oh my God!" I exclaim forgetting she'd recognize my voice.

"Bruno!" she yells. She runs out.

I run after her. I need to comfort her, give her my support, and figure out what we'll do together.

"Fabiola!" I yell.

She won't stop. She's running across the street when the car hits her. I run to her side. The impact was so hard…it killed her instantly…

THE WRITER FROM HELL
(FOREWORD)

A famous writer who was hiding his identity using the pseudonym, The Writer from Hell, is recognized internationally. During his career, he has published many books, listed as being damned. No one knows his true identity, but he has decided to show the public his face for the first time with the release of his latest novel, ANGEL GABRIEL'S RAPE,"

A priest, with a peaceful life in his parish, will find himself trapped in the eye of the hurricane. His relationship with The Writer from Hell is exposed. Showing people that good and evil can have the same face.

* THE WRITER OF HELL *

It was on the front page of every newspaper around the country. Big black bold letters read, "THE WRITER FROM HELL and ANGEL GABRIEL'S RAPE," the picture they used showed two faces facing one another, as if challenging each other. Everyone spoke about what had occurred. TV shows, radio stations, viewers and listeners calling non-stop to give their opinion on the matter.

The numerous phone calls to my parish and cell had me fed up. No one called about anything related to the parish. All anyone was interested in was the book, I even had to cancel any activities related to the parish. People came from all over to mass, to watch me, snap photos. I didn't recognize any faces, these weren't my parishioners. Some looked at me with curiosity, mockingly, pity.

All the pressure pushed me to ask Father David Contreras, the vicar, to watch over the parish for some time. While I sorted this whole thing out as best as I could. I didn't even know if there was a way out of all this.

The Writer From Hell. What was he thinking when he chose that name? Why is he so fixated on writing about such dark things? Why did he insist on attacking the church, while being a priest? Did he ever imagine his books would have the impact they had? How did he feel when he heard people saying his books were cursed?

Those are the kinds of question everyone wanted the answers to. They wanted to get the answers from my mouth. I knew I could keep continue this much longer, living as if I'd committed a crime. The people wouldn't rest until they got the answers they wanted. I was going to go ahead and hold an interview.

Before I could go through with said interview. I must first be granted permission from Bishop Monsignor Francis Xavier Penilla. I needed his ok and I wanted his advise on how to deal with such a sensitive issue. I requested to meet with him.

I disguised myself when I went to meet with the Bishop. I wore dark sunglasses, a mustache, long sleeve turtle neck (despite how hot it was), and a baseball cap. This measures were necessary, I didn't want anyone to recognize me, especially a reporter. They'd immediately pull out recording devices and bombard me with questions. As soon as I was safely in, I strip my disguise. The bishop kindly greets me, "Good morning father Julian. How're you?" he asks extending his hand to me, which I lean over to kiss.

"Good morning Monsignor, I'm still processing everything that is happening. It's unbelievable how my life has drastically changed overnight. I was just another priest, an average Joe, now I'm the center of attention. It's not something I like or wish upon anyone."

"I understand. It's not an easy situation. Rest assured that you're not alone. All of us are here for you, we're praying so the Lord can help you get through this."

"Thank you so much Monsignor. It means a lot to me to know that. I've come here today to see you because I'd like you to grant me permission to offer the everyone an interview. I feel pressured and honestly I feel like it's time I talk."

"You have my permission father Julian. You're not guilty of what's occurring, you simply are the victim of unfortunate circumstances. I just ask you pick the most credible news program. Be yourself, straightforward, say what you know and nothing else."

"I will do that Monsignor. I'll say exactly what I know and how things happened. I'd also like to ask for your permission to take some time off to be alone. I need to reflect on what happened, find peace, and try to let everyone forget what has occurred. When people stop seeing your face on TV they tend to forget you even exist."

"I understand father Julian, take the time you need. All I ask is that you keep in touch, update me of your whereabouts, and how you are. May God be with you."

He gives me his blessing and I leave the bishopric. I needed to find who I wanted to give an interview to.

Had it been up to me I would've never touched the subject. But deep down inside I knew that sooner or later I would have to deal with this. So I decided to take the advise the bishop gave me, be straightforward, say what I knew, and pray that soon this would all be over.

Monsignor received many letters, questioning him as to how he could still have me as a priest in his diocese.

I decided to have Ruben del Rincon interview me, he seem to be the one people could take more seriously. He had a reputation of being honest, transparent, and sincere. I called his secretary and we scheduled the interview.

The interview would be streaming live. I arrived at the station about 10 minutes before I was to begin. The director told me that I might need to stay more than the hour, being as he didn't believe we could cover everything in that amount of time. I made no promises. I avoided talking to anyone, I didn't want to see whether they had a list of questions prepared for me, I wasn't interested in make up. I'd been told that anyone who is to come on TV needs their make up done, these things were insignificant to me. My sole purpose for being there, was to show everyone who I was, a simple and ordinary priest. Who unfortunately found himself in the eye of a hurricane at the moment.

"We're on in 5...4...3..."

I think they meant I am on a blinking light and ask God that everything goes well.

"Good afternoon and welcome to, The Aftermath. Good afternoon father Julian, thank you for this interview."

"Good afternoon Ruben."

"Let's get straight to the point. In this talkshow as you may already know, we speak with honesty and sincerity. So with no further ado, how long have you known of the existence of The Writer from Hell?"

"When the first book was shipped to my house, it was autographed and I believed it to be a gift from a friend."

"He signed the first book and you didn't recognize the handwriting?"

"His writing isn't much different from other writers."

"How long have you known the identity of The Writer from Hell?"

"I'm sorry, can I ask you to not call him by that name?"

"I'm sorry father, but he is the one who came up with the pseudonym. That's how he signed all his books. No one knew his real name or what he look like up until last week. Can you answer my question please, how long have you known the identity of The Writer from Hell?"

"I found out who he was, one day before the release his latest book. Meaning I knew one day before the public knew."

"You mean to tell me, that you never suspected what his real identity was?"

"No Ruben, I didn't. At first I heard of his books because many of the people from my church often came to me looking for answers related to the stories he wrote. I received his first book some times after, once done reading it I continued reading the others."

"I'm sorry father, it's just a little hard to believe that you never suspected anything seeing the kind of relationship you had."

"Look Ruben, I think it is more than evident that he was very good at keeping his identity secret. We had a great relationship, anytime I needed his help he was there for me. We didn't live together, and the times that we did see each other, we usually spoke about me. How I felt in my parish, about how people followed me, how I was feeling, whether I was happy. Anytime I tried asking about him he simply said, he was fine and happy and not to worry about him. He always seemed ok."

"Did he ever mentioned to you, that he was a writer?"

"No, and the times I was in his home I didn't see anything that's lead me to believe that he was."

"What did you guys talk about the day before the release of his latest book?"

"I will tell you because we spoke in the sacristy but not in secret of confession.

He told me he needed to see me, that he had something very urgent and sensitive to discuss with me. It was the first time he'd ever said anything like this to me so I became worried. I pulled out a bottle of red wine to offer him while we spoke. He arrived punctually, as usual.

"Julian, how are you?"

We hugged and he began to talk…

"Tell me something Julian, what do you think of the book, THE ONE WHO MOST LOVED HIM?"

"You're here to discuss one of the books, that The Writer From Hell wrote?" I asked confused.

"Please Julian, just answer my question, what do you think of the book?"

"I don't believe that it's a book that should've been published. People aren't ready to read that kind of stuff. I know it's just a fictional novel, but you have no idea how many people have come to me asking if what's written in the book is true. Honestly I feel the only reason he would write about such a thing is to become more famous."

"Really? Is that what you think about the writer? That he only seeks fame?"

"Juan I don't really see this conversation getting us anywhere. Why don't we talk about you instead?"

"Did you read, YOU DECIDE, NOT HIM?"

"Yes, there was a lot of suicide cases after the release of that book. It clearly relayed the message that suicide was the answer to our problems. How could the writer say that we are in control of when we die, not God."

"How many of his books have you read?"

"Unfortunately, I've had to read them all. With so many people constantly coming to me with questions about them, I needed to be informed, know what they were talking about."

"Can you describe the books to me in your own words?"

"BELOVED DARK ANGEL" clearly promotes Satanic cults. I don't think the author realized just how many people would put into practice what he wrote must be done to bond with a demon. Maybe this was just a means to get his career going. Unfortunately when someone writes about something so serious people tend to believe it to be true.
"THE MESSENGER", you could say is a prequel that also promotes satanic cults. It claims that Satan's reigning is fast approaching, it's absurd. Satan will never reign over God.
"DARK SECRETS" was an outright book of lies. Since he spoke of events that proved the reigning of Satan was coming.
"SACRILEGIOUS", speaks of something many right about. It focuses on the negative aspects of the church.
"LIBERATION" this one shows me that he is capable of writing anything to sell his books, either that or he simply isn't right in the head. How can he encourage substance abuse as a means to deal with life's problems.

His latest book, I have no idea as to what it's about but I expect the worse from it."

"ANGEL GABRIEL'S RAPE," is the name of the book"

"How do you know? Don't tell me you also read his books. I've never seen one in your home or with you."

ANGEL GABRIEL'S RAPE," has been promoted for about 3 weeks now. It's already broken Guinness records and it hasn't even been released. Book stores and libraries have already ordered thousands of copies. Everyone anxiously awaits it's release, more than with all other books. The Writer From Hell announced this will be his last book and that for that very reason he'd be revealing his identity. Countless death threats have been made."

"How do you know all this? I've heard of everything but not the death threats. Where'd you get that information?"

He stares at me very seriously. Took a sip from the glass of wine and calmly said, "I know for the simple reason that…

I am The Writer From Hell."

He looked me straight in the eyes.

"What're you saying?!? This is a terrible joke."

"Unfortunately it's not. This why I wanted to meet with you. I needed to tell you what the book is about."

He explained to me what it was about. I begged him to halt the release of the book. He couldn't release such a horrific story. It was his biggest attack against God yet. He'd put his life at risk once people read it, and he'd be taking me down with him once his identity was known. He was practically forcing me to give up my life as a priest. I tried to get him to understand, but all he said was:

"Julian, people must understand that we are two different individuals. They will see that you have chosen to live a life of priesthood and that you believe in God unconditionally. I don't, there's no reason why you should pay for my mistakes."

"Do you really think it's that simple? People won't see it that way! I would have a hard time differentiating myself. What you've written is insane! You can't release ANGEL GABRIEL'S RAPE," At least stay anonymous. I'm begging you."

"I'm sorry Julian. There's no turning back now. Everything is set. I'd like for you to be at the book release tomorrow, but I know it's asking a bit much of you, so I won't pressure you. I'll let you decide."

Like that he ended our conversation, finished his glass of wine, hugged me and left. I stayed there, trying to process it all. Get my thoughts in order.

I arrive to the auditorium where the release is set to take place. There's an immense amount of people, it's astonishing to see just how many people want to see who this anonymous writer is. I manage to get to the front row. I still had hope he wouldn't show up, bit he did.

He was dressed very elegantly, in all black. He was dressed as a priest. It was ridiculous to me. I'm sure most people thought that he was a priest. He walked tall and confidently with his book in hand. He grabbed the microphone and said:

"Welcome ladies and gentlemen. good afternoon. Thank you so much for coming to this event, your presence is very important to me. Alot of you have shown to be loyal readers of mine. My name is Juan Castellanos, I am The Writer From Hell!!"

The people gave him a standing ovation and began applauding. Posters with the cover of the book were lit up all around. "ANGEL GABRIEL'S RAPE," was written in red cursive letters. The cover was black with wings on it, you could see innocent eyes within the wings. On the bottom of the cover, "The Writer From Hell" was written small.

My God. I thought to myself, in what moment did he come up with the story?
The lights from the camera flashes were like lightning. Then our eyes met.
The events that followed felt as if happening in slow motion…

I walk up to the stage. Everyone looked at me as if I were a madman. Maybe I had lost my sanity, I was interrupting the most anticipated event. I was walking towards him when I felt the floor spinning. I didn't understand what was happening.
I embraced him to keep myself from falling. He was well aware that the floor had a rotating center. It was so the audience could see him from all angles. He embraced me back.

Once the spinning stopped he bent down to pick up his book that had fallen. I see him look up about to speak, I assumed he wanted to explain his relationship to me. I was a mirror image of him. I thought he had maybe gotten dizzy, but once he fell to the floor and I saw the blood I understood what had happened. Someone shot him in the chest with a gun, clearly they had attach a silencer to it. I dropped to the floor and take him in my arms. I saw the life leaving his body, and there's was nothing I could do to help. My tears fall onto his body."

"Everyone saw him was for something into your ear, what did he say?"

"Four words, four words was all he could say:

Forgive me my brother."

"What does that mean to you father, to be the brother of The Writer From Hell?"

"Before anything, to me he was my brother, my blood. Just like to a mother no child can be seen as evil. The same applied to me when it came to my brother. To me, Juan was not a bad person. He simply expressed what he felt through his writings, that was a right that no one could deny him. No one was forced to read his books."

"Why is it that no one knew about your twin brother?"

"We never tried keeping it a secret, our relatives and friends knew. He lived in a different city and we didn't see each other often. It's just that now that he is the famous anonymous author and I'm a priest, everyone found out."

"Is there anything you would like to add?"

"Yes, I ask that you let my brother rest in peace. Do not judge him. He is not here to defend himself or answer the many questions we had for him."

"Well folks, there you have it. Unfortunately we are all at a time. Father Julian I'd like to thank you again for coming in today to talk to us. Again, our condolences for the death of your brother Juan."

"No, Ruben, thank you for having me. Allowing me to explain myself."

I sneak into a restroom. Put on the fake mustache, sunglasses, cap, and coat. So no one will recognize me. I get into a taxi, and plan to travel using different ones in case someone's following me. My phone vibrates and I see the name of my representative, best friend, and accomplice, Francisco Ambriz, on the screen. It's a text message:

"I was beginning to worry for you. Amazing how everything went according to plan, genius is move dropping the book and letting your brother bend over to pick it up. Without a doubt the killer would think that only the author would be so quick to pick up his masterpiece from the floor. So tell me what's next?"

I reply: "I have the rough draft for the next book, I will be sending it out to you soon. If the world thinks that ANGEL GABRIEL'S RAPE," was the worst thing I had written wait till they read, "THOMAS, THE TWIN".

SOMETHING MORE

In every day life, things tend to happen that we can't explain. Life changes in a matter of seconds, sometimes it's as though we are just chess pieces in a game.

Many say that reality exceeds fantasy. I agree with that statement. I present to you a series of stories of ordinary people, in situations that might seem unrealistic but nevertheless somewhere in the world maybe even in your own life could happen...

CHILD FULL OF GRACE

I look at my clock and see that 25 minutes have gone by. I pulled my car up to the entrance of the restaurant turn on my hazard lights and get off. I look into the restaurant, there's a lot of people waiting to be sat.

I see my wife walk out the restroom with the child and her arms. Yes! She'd been able to do it.

I see to one of the waitresses and say, "Excuse me my wife needs me to help her with her son" she lets me through.

"She was changing his diaper, and left him for a moment to go into the restroom. I didn't hesitate and took him before she noticed. Come on let's hurry before she does."

"Perfect" I respond. I was full of joy, we'd done it once again. At this rate we'd be rich soon and be able to retire.

We hurried out the restaurant, got into the car, and it quickly drive off.

I drive to the "clinic" on 15th St. where they get the children ready.

Once at the clinic, the guy in charge comes out, he recognizes us and says, "Hey guys, how're you? Nice to see you again. We need more people like you around here, you keep us busy."

"We brought a boy this time."

"Give me the boy, will take care of him while you guys go get your paperwork ready."

We drive to the house, I stop by the gas station to fill up my tank. I buy a pack of cigarettes. Although we've been doing this for a while, sometimes my nerves get the best of me, the cigarettes help.

We got everything together, and got a phone call from the clinic letting us know that the boy was ready about an hour after dropping him off.

When we arrived at the clinic, they had a child and say, "He's still sleeping so hurry."

We leave our car at the clinic and take a taxi to the border. We would cross walking, once in the US we take a taxi to Laredo, then a bus to San Antonio Texas. There a good amount of money awaited us.

It's our turn. My wife hands her green card and a birth certificate for the boy to the officer. She briefly lifts the blanket to show him the baby and tells him that he sleeping. I hand him my green card, after the search us, right as we're about to walk through, we hear a yell.

"That's my baby! Stop them! They have my baby!"

We both look up to see her and a man running towards us.

"They're taking my son, that's his blanket! I knit it for him!"

How could we have overlooked that? M

The officer stops us. My wife is about to hand over the baby, when the woman tears him away from her. Our cover was blown…

"Noooooo! My baby! What did you do to him?!?! Oh my God!"

The blanket exposed the scar on his abdomen, right above the diaper. She shook him, attempting to wake him up, but it was all in vain…

His body was full with drugs.

Immediately we were arrested. We didn't even try to resist.

The thing we were still on Mexican territory and with a good lump of money we'd be out of jail in no time.

GOD'S TELEPHONE NUMBER

Sometimes children ask questions that make us laugh. Sometimes they ask questions that frustrate us. Sometimes they ask questions that make us cry.

"What's God's phone number?"

That's the question my nephew Brandon, 4 years old at the time, asked me a few years ago.

It was Sunday, October 16, 2005. Vale, my younger brother had gone to Mexico, along with my mom, Brandon, Jasmine (my 1 year old niece), and his wife Isela.

A little after 2 AM on Tuesday, October 18, they got into a tragic accident in San Luis Potosí, Mexico. Unfortunately in this accident, my sister-in-law lost her life.

The days after her death were difficult. It was extremely difficult and painful to see my brother try to move on with his two children who were constantly asking,

"Where's my mommy?"

"When is mommy coming home?"

The answer we gave them…"She's with God."

My brother moved into my parents home, where I was also living. This way we'd be able to help him with the children

One night, after I get home from work, I find Brandon with the phone in his hand. He had learned to call my brother on it a few days ago, and he'd constantly dial him. My brother was in Mexico and I assumed he was attempting to call his cell phone. I say to him, "Hang up the phone sweetheart, your dad will be back soon."

His next words, hurt deep within my soul...

"Uncle Ben, I'm not trying to call my daddy. I want to call God. Do you know his number?"

"Why do you want to talk to God?" I asked

"I want to talk to my mommy. I want to ask her when she's coming home because I miss her a lot."

I couldn't fight back the tears. I hug him and tell him his mom is with God, but that when he closed his eyes to sleep he'd see his mom with him.

A few days go by, when my niece, Jasmine. asked me the same thing.

"Uncle Ben, what's God's number?"

Brandon responds, "God doesn't have a number. Right uncle Ben? When you close your eyes and go to sleep, you will see her."

It's been eight years since my sister-in-law's death. My brother has remarried, and my nephew and niece continue to grow. The memory of hearing my nephew ask me that question still pains me.

"What's God's telephone number?"

THE GRADUATION

Although I had the AC on, it was so hot, I had cold sweat running down my back.

Everything started last night.

It's 7:45, the ceremony is scheduled to start at 8:00. There's not a car in sight on the main road. Everyone must already be at California High School.

California is a small town in central Missouri. It has just over 2000 inhabitants. Aside from being a quiet town, its people have a reputation for being very hospitable and punctual. Something I still have to work on.

I get to the streetlight on 87th Ave. and 50th Hwy., to my bad luck I catch the red light. I should've left my apartment with more time.

I take off as soon as the light turns green. I'm driving a Grand Vitara Suzuki. I drive quickly past the stores and mini mall.

I'm approaching the Dollar General store, when I see a boy in a blue cap and gown racing down the street. He must be one of the graduates and is running late. I pull up next to him.

"Hey I'm heading to California High, need a lift?"

He turned and looked surprised at first, he hops into my car.

"Hey, my name is Ben. One of my nieces is graduating today, her name is Yesenia."

"Hey, I am Dwight Callaway, I must not know her. I can't remember any girl by that name."

"Well I'm sure there's a lot of students graduating. Besides she's a very quite girl."

"My parents left before me so they could find their seats. I came in my car but was stranded two blocks back. My parents promise to give me a car as my graduation gift, because I was accepted and got a scholarship to go study at Missouri University. Here's my letter of acceptance."

He pulls out a white envelope with the school logo on it. It was the most well known and prestigious school in the state.

What's little strange to me is that he doesn't seem happy, he had a sad look. You'd expect someone who has made such a great achievement to be happy.

I put to the school, the place is full. I pull over so Dwight can get off while I go find parking.

When I finally reached the auditorium it's full to its maximum capacity. One of the ushers hands me a pearl gray brochure with the school logo and name on it in turquoise letters. "California High School Graduating Class of 2010" it reads.

I sit down and start going through the names of the graduates listed on the brochure. I find my niece's, Yesenia Guillén. I can't seem to find Dwight's.

Maybe I misunderstood his name. Or maybe I just don't know how to spell it.

I decided to just pay attention to see when he is called up so I can see how to write his name.

The orchestra begins to play. The graduates walk in couples. One boy one girl. With their blue caps and gowns, the girls hold a white flower. I didn't see Dwight.

The professors begin their welcoming speeches, they call up the students who are top of the class up for special diplomas. A sense of pride overcomes me when I hear my niece's name mentioned.

Afterwards each student gets called up one by one to get there at school diploma. I pay close attention to see when Dwight get called up. I see my niece walk up for her diploma but never see Dwight walk up to the stage. Then I think about how my niece told me that some students are allowed to attend the graduation but aren't allowed to walk because of missing credits. They aren't given their diploma until they've met all requirements. This couldn't be his case, he said he was going away for college.

The ceremony ends and the graduates throw up their caps, as they come down pigeons are released to fly away.

Everyone is taking pictures when I find my niece, I hand her a gift I took for her, hug her and took a few pictures with her.

I tell her about the guy had picked off the street. Mention his name to her, but she tells me there's no one by that name in the school.

I drive my knees home and head to my apartment. I can't stop thinking about Dwight. It was so weird that I hadn't seen him in the ceremony. When I arrived to my apartment and park my car I see the white envelope in my passenger seat. I pick it up and recognize the Missouri University logo.

Dwight Callaway
701 Ryan Street
California, Missouri

What's going on?

I decide that I'll wait till morning to return the envelope. It was late and a lot of the graduates had gone out with their families to celebrate.

The next morning I wake up early, shower and put on a light pair shorts and shirt. It's going to be very hot. I head for Dwight's house.

Ryan Street is at the edge of town. I saw the White House with a large green tree outside. The mailbox read:

701 Ryan Street
Callaway Family

I ring the doorbell and I'll thin woman answers. She was a thin, wore a navy skirt, and a white blouse, over it a white apron. Her hair was up in a ponytail with some loose strands. Her eyes are sad, I realize who Dwight inherited the sad look from.

"Good morning young man, can I help you with something?"

"Good morning, I'm looking for Dwight."

Her becomes pale instantly. She completely opens the door and invites me in. Then calls to her husband.

"Honey, can you come to the living room please?"

A man of a stocky built entered the room, he was wearing black jeans, and a red and white plaid shirt, with black boots. He must've been around 60, maybe a little too old to be Dwight's father.

"Sweetheart, this gentleman is asking for Dwight. Do you mind talking with him please? I'm going to make some more lemonade it's a little hot."

"Good morning, my name is Blake Callaway."

"Good morning, I'm Ben Guillén."

"How can I help you, young man?"

I explained everything that happened the day before. How I found Dwight walking down the street and gave him a ride to the graduation ceremony, but didn't see his name on the brochure or walking the stage. That I later on found his acceptance letter in my vehicle."

"Wait a minute, are you saying my son was with you yesterday?"

She takes the picture and hands it to me, "Please look at it closely, are you sure this is the young man you speak of?"

It's a picture of Dwight. He's wearing a baseball uniform, it's the sport of choice in California. His blue eyes stand out, he looks like a different person when he smiles.

"Yes this is him. Why?"

"Can I see the letter you speak of?"

I handed it to her, she opens it and starts crying as she reads it.

"12 years ago yesterday, my son Dwight was getting ready for his graduation ceremony. He was delighted because he had been accepted to Missouri University of Columbia. My wife and I left to the ceremony before him so we could find some seats. He never arrived.
He was driving his car passed the Dollar General store when he got into a car accident that killed him. The other vehicle was driving at a very high speed and hit him head-on.
We never been able to find this letter that you brought us today."

Although I had the AC on, it was so hot, I had cold sweat running down my back.

WITHERED ROSES

He breathed deeply several times, thinking about what awaited him after he crossed that door. He was shaking. On more than one occasion the thought of retrieving crossed his mind, but imagining the sadness on his brother's and sister's faces if he were to show up home empty handed gave him courage to push through what he was about to do. He gathered courage and told himself, "come on Carlos, this is not your first time."

Before touching the door knob he looked once more at the strip. He saw large, brightly lit ornaments hanging on poles; it didn't feel like night time. There are still hawkers on the street, children cleaning windshields, others selling packs of gum, and others who are more like Carlos, selling bouquets, but not one person stopped his car to make a purchase. Everyone was in a hurry, because of the television announcement, stores are having a Christmas super sale and it will end at 10:00 PM. A few minutes were all that is left so his hope of being able to sell roses has vanished.

Putting his fears aside, he knocked on the door and a greasy haired man opened it.

"Come in, Carlos." He said with a smile. "It's been a while since you last visited me. I thought you must have forgotten me already. Someday, you might come knocking and I won't open."

Carlos peered at him; he was a thin man with dark, long and very thin hair. He had sharp nose like that of a preying bird, small black eyes that resembled those of a mouse, bushy eyebrows and missing some teeth. His smile was more like a grimace. It was difficult to guess his age, but he appeared to be over fifty years old. He was dressed entirely in black; he resembled one of those guys in stories that were responsible for burying the dead.

Attempting to overcome the fear that he had for this man, he smiled back. Carlos entered the house and the door closed behind him.

Along with the door, any hopes that he would be unscathed in that house also close. He promised himself that he will not weep, that he will not give this repugnant being the pleasure of seeing him cry and beg. Once again, he gathered the courage he needed and prepared himself to endure being used like a rag doll...

No sooner had he crossed the middle of the room when the guy spins Carlos around, looks at him from head to toe, instructs him to kneel before him. The guy pulled down his pants and told Carlos, "begin."

Carlos opened his mouth and closed his eyes. He let the guy take control; he held his head and pushes and pulls Carlos' head toward and away from his crotch. Carlos lets his imagination take over, it is his way of escaping this scene. His body is being used and degraded by this heartless degenerate. Carlos refuses though, to let himself be affected. He will not complain; the guy could use his body, cause him bodily pain but he could never harm his heart...

Carlos saw himself in a faraway place, a place he had never been. This was the place that his mother described in her stories when he was still a five year old boy, before his mother was beaten to death by his drunken father.

This place was impressive, it is full of fruit trees, there are animals of all species and they ran everywhere in the forest. It seemed to him that all the animals were all friends, there were no feuds between dogs and cats. He saw a lion playing with a small sheep, an eagle trying to teach a newborn chick how to fly, and a chimpanzee riding on the back of a wolf…

Carlos saw the images again and again and wondered if someday he could visit this place.

After his father had beat his mother to death during one of his many drunken rages, he fled, leaving Carlos, then an 8 year old boy, to fend and provide the needs of his 4 year old brother and 2 year old sister.

Carlos had fled with his brother and sister when he overheard from a neighbor that the government would be taking them in. He was afraid that they would all be separated. He found a space on dumping grounds where a lady, known as "la jefa (the boss)" let him build a sort of room, with pieces of cardboard and foil, where he and his siblings would sleep in.

It had been six years since then and Carlos, now 14 years old, matured quickly with blows and suffering, despite still being almost a child, he was very strong. He did not show his feelings to anyone other than to his siblings. He wouldn't allow anyone to cheat him and he was like a lion when defending himself and his siblings. He had grown up to be strong and attractive, which got him a lot of attention from women as well as from men. This helped him discover that he could make money in ways other than by selling roses.

The first time he did this was when he was only 10 years old. He remembered the experience to be very painful, but the most painful thing was to see the guy laughing as he watched

Carlos crying. It hurt so much to see that man mocking him with laughter; it was after that he swore to himself that he would never again let anyone see him cry. He would be strong and hard as a rock and only in extreme cases would he agree to that kind of trade.

And that night had been one of those extreme cases. He had spent the whole day attempting to sell roses. Going from one street to the next, traffic light to traffic light but nobody bought one bouquet of roses. Several times he had to find some source of water to dampen the roses as they'd start to wither away; making them even harder to sell. With every passing hour, the roses withered more and more and with the withered roses, withered his hopes of being able to sell.

"Come on, moan…" The guy said. "Moan and tell me that you like it."

He did what he said; he needed to make the man happy, even though he was far from being pleased with what was happening. When the guy finally climaxed, he pulled away from the guy. He reached for the money the guy extended his hand and said,

"I like what you did tonight; you were good, and since it's almost Christmas. I'll give you extra; you've earned it."

"Thanks." It was the only word he said and left the house.

It hurt to walk, but he didn't show it. He pretended he didn't feel anything and just went out through the door.

Closing the door behind him, he saw the wilted roses which he dropped before entering the house. He thought of picking it up, but changed his mind. He wanted this disgusting being to see them the next day when he stepped out his house. So he'd realize that because of them he was able to sleep with someone who was still almost a child.

All because of withered roses...

KAPLAN

Upon entering the restaurant, I felt how all the eyes drawn towards me. Damn, people were confusing me with him again.

A waiter dressed in black slacks, a white shirt, black tie and black shoes approached me, I smiled and he said, "Welcome to La Siesta Mr. Kaplan, follow me please."

He took me to a table away from the appreciating looks of the other customers.

I was sick of being confused with the famous actor Ben Kaplan. I looked in the mirror and although the resemblance was downright amazing, I had my own life, my own dreams and goals in life. I wanted to be myself and stop feeling like the shadow of another person. There was no place in the city where I was not received differently. Always greeted with a, "Welcome Mr. Kaplan".

I ate without slowly, I didn't have much of an appetite. Even the tequila which the owner of the restaurant gave as his complimentary gift failed to excite me. I tried to be as nice as my discomfort allowed me to and left the restaurant thereafter.

I had only walked a couple of blocks when I saw him.

He was dressed entirely in black. His coat fell to mid-calf and close necked; disabling anybody from seeing if he's wearing anything underneath. A hat partially covered his face; his profile seemed vaguely familiar but I couldn't point from where.

He was leaning against the wall, smoking quietly as he watched the moon. When he heard my footsteps, he turned to me.

"Kaplan, how are you?" He said, still smoking. "I saw you having dinner inside the restaurant but I don't want to interrupt. Do you want to have a cigarette?"

"Thanks, sir but I don't smoke." I replied.

"What? Don't tell me that not only have you forgotten my name and opted to address me as 'sir'. But that you've also quit smoking? Kaplan, I think you're really sick. You really need to take a break and spend time alone. Fortunately, we are about to finish filming the movie and then you can take a long and well-deserved vacation. Oh by the way, the place you've recommended for the ending of the film is great. Tomorrow we'll be going there along with all the equipment and once we're done filming, all will be great. Here's your card back with the address of the cabin you gave me, I already noted it in my schedule as well. On another note, I like your new way of addressing me."

I took the card from him and before I could say a word he walked away towards the bars.

I took the card, looked at the address and decided to visit the place. I did not know that Ben Kaplan was in town, let alone that he's filming a movie here. Now I understood why people confused me with him more than the usual! Tonight I would go to see the place, to check out what type of cabin Kaplan had recommended. Tomorrow night, I'll be there as well. I bet everyone will be shocked to see me and the real Kaplan; I bet that would be such an unforgettable experience for everyone.

I walked to the taxi stand and before I could even say anything, the window opened and a smiling blond girl with stunning blue eyes and radiant smile said,

"Mr. Kaplan! What a pleasant surprise." She then called one of their taxi drivers. "Please sit down."

I hadn't even taken a seat when a young man of about 22 years of age appeared and said to me,

"Mr. Kaplan, I will be your driver for tonight. Where do you want me to take you?"

Once inside the taxi, I gave him the card. The driver read it and said:

"Are you sure, Mr. Kaplan? People say that this place is cursed. I see you don't have anyone with you. Would you like for us to have pick somebody up to accompany you?"

I wanted to laugh out loud but I suppressed myself. Stories about haunted places almost always amuse me. Smiling, I replied,

"Don't worry, my friend. I know the place well and there's also friends already waiting for me there."

The driver looked at me with eyes full of wonder. Then he shrugged and drove in silence. We drove for about 20 minutes and then the taxi driver told me,

"Mr. Kaplan, this is as far as I am able to take you. I can't drive further because the road to the cabin must be done on foot. I have a lamp here; you can use it to illuminate your way and you can just return it tomorrow. Don't worry about the payment;

expenses are paid for by the company." He handed me the lamp, shook my hands and drove off.

The cabin looked gloomier than I initially expected it to. The fact that it was far from the village, was surrounded with trees and could only be reached on foot made it creepier.

The moon peeked shyly through the clouds, I took the lamp the taxi driver lent me and I entered the stone path to reach the cabin. There was no light, it was pitch black, the door was ajar so I pushed a little and walked inside.

I took maybe two steps when I felt something pounce on my body, I fell forward and hit my head against the wooden floor. I immediately tasted blood in my mouth. I realized that the light from the flash light must've warned whoever was in the cabin of my arrival. I knew that it was rude of me not to knock first, but I don't think striking me is justifiable.

Well, everything inside was dark and whoever it is who pounced on me couldn't see my face. Perhaps if he or she had recognized me as Kaplan I wouldn't have been greeted like this. I decided to apologize for my intrusion. My train of thought was interrupted by another sharp blow to my head and I lost consciousness...

When I regained consciousness, I was felt a terrible headache. Someone poured a bucket of ice water all over me. It took me a few minutes before I began to remember what happened. I was sitting in a chair, my hand and feet were bound and my clothes were stripped from me except my black boxer. I saw a small lamp on a table in a corner which gave off a dim light to the room. I turned my head left and right and I saw a single cabinet; I couldn't see anybody.

"I already warned you not to come back here or I would punish you." A voice I felt coming from a man behind me said. "But I can see that you're very insistent. Now I can't risk releasing you as you might be reporting me to the police. I will have to silence you."

"Who are you?" I asked. "We haven't talked before. I came here because…"

"Silence!" Said the man and he placed a handkerchief over my mouth so I could not speak. He went around to sit in a chair and face me. That's when I saw him: he must be about six feet in height, sturdily built, extremely short hair, small eyes that looked insane. He was wearing a scary smile and in his hand was a huge double-edged sword.

Without uttering a word, he plunged the knife in my abdomen; the pain I felt was unbearable and I howled, but the scarf covering my mouth did a great job of stifling the cry. He turned the knife looking to make the most possible damage; I felt my insides ripping. Then he pulled the knife out of my body and plunged the same knife on my chest. I fell back and I felt confused as to what happened next…

I stood up, over him. Watching this man bent over me as he pulled the knife out of my body. I heard him mutter, "too easy, you didn't last long at all." He then proceeded to cut my body. All of a sudden he stops and jumps to his feet. He runs behind the door. A light comes in from outside. I looked out the window and see a guy walking casually toward the cabin, carrying a lamp in hand and despite the darkness, I could see his face…he looks just like me. It was him…Kaplan!

I yell, I'm sure of it, but he did not hear me. He just continues walking…

HERO

I looked down at my watch and saw the time, it was 4:25 PM.

I was in line at the bank, I needed to make a deposit otherwise there wouldn't be enough funds in my account to cover all the automatic payments that were going to go through. The bank would be closing at 4:30 PM and the man in front of me was taking forever to complete his transaction with the cashier.

"Sir, please proceed to my desk," an elegant young woman says to me. She was seated next to the cashier I waiting in line for.

"Thank you very much, ma'am," I said. "You don't understand how much I appreciate you assisting me, I urgently need to make this deposit and…"

"Wait. Don't I know you? Yes! I could never forget your face, you left without giving me a chance to thank you that day, I must tell you, you are a hero!"

Confused I say, "excuse me, ma'am, I think you've mistaken me for someone else. I don't know you and I'm no hero. I'm just a car salesman. I've never done anything heroic"

"I'm sure it's you, but let's talk about that later. Can I have your ID please?" she says.

I hand her my I.D. and explain to her what I need. She looks at me carefully and she proceeds to complete the transaction.

I watch her quietly. She was so focused on what she was doing she didn't notice that I was scrutinizing her. She is tall, slim, her hair pulled back in a bun on top of her head. She has a small nose, a small mouth, gray eyes and a mole on her neck...

The mole on her neck...Wait, I've seen that mole before!

The memories flood my mind suddenly and it all came back to me. It involved an event that I wanted to bury in my memory. It came back harder than ever, reminding me that I was once a piece of garbage, a degenerate being and definitely not a hero as she claimed.

Six years ago...

I was out with high school friends. I had finished high school two years before but had some friends who were graduating at that time and they called me up to celebrate. It was Friday and it was already getting dark.

I went out together with my three friends: George, Sebastian and Fernando. We went to a bar and started drinking beer. After a while, we started smoking pot and we felt like we were masters of the world.

"Hey guys," George said. "I heard Silvia was waiting in the park for her boyfriend. I say we go find her and invite her to join us?

"I doubt she would accept that," Sebastian replied. "Silvia strikes me as a serious and studious type. Let's think of someone else."

"I agree with George, Silvia has always loved her boyfriend, but, I've always found her quite attractive and we could probably convince her. If she refuses, well, that'll be her mistake. What do you think Sergio, shall we?"

I just say yes.

We were laughing on our way to the park with beers in hand. Upon arrival, I saw a girl sitting on a bench and based on my friends' reaction could tell that it was Silvia. She was indeed very lovely. Jorge approached her very quietly from behind and hit her on the head suddenly; the girl fainted and Jorge carried her in his arms. We took her to a dimly lit street where we knew that there was little foot traffic. There, under the influence of beer and marijuana, we raped her.

When I finished the vile act, I felt like the worst man in the world. As Jorge and Sebastian raped her, she began to awaken.

"Hey, the doll has opened her eyes," Jorge said. "This is could be a problem. If we're recognized, she'll report us to the authorities. We will have to kill her!"

After saying that, they began to beat her. Without thinking twice or any hesitation, I dialed the emergency number on my phone and ran to stop them.

"Have you all gone mad?" I screamed at them. "Just leave her there, don't do anything."

"Looks like this coward needs a beating as well." Jorge told Fernando. While Jorge was occupied with beating the girl, Fernando and Sebastian turned to me and started to beat me. A few moments later, police sirens were heard. They fled in haste and I took the opportunity to get closer to the girl.

"Are you alright? Please don't move. The police are here." As I held her head, she opened her eyes and looked at me.

"Thank you," she said in a whisper. "You're a hero; you saved my life."

The police came and an ambulance was called. They determined that I had saved the girl. She told them that I was the one who had saved her from her assailants. We were taken to the hospital to receive treatment. After I was treated I told the authorities that if they needed me for their investigation, they could simply give me a call. I gave them my information and left. A few days later, I was told by the police that the girl wouldn't file any charges. She figured rapists were rarely caught so there was no point. I felt a huge sense of relief and regret at the same time.

I decided to move to the other end of town; I also decided never to see Sebastian, Jorge and Fernando because they had proven that they were capable of anything, even attacking a friend. I was determined to change for the better, to be a good man and not to harm any woman again.

"Are you all right, sir?"

Silvia's voice snapped me out of my memories.

"Yes. Why?" I ask.

"I asked you if there's anything else that you wanted me to do. You didn't answer and you keep looking at me. I'm pretty sure you remember me now. I would like to invite you for a dinner at my house tonight. Would you join me?"

"Alright," I replied. "I'd be happy to."

Once finished at work, she told me, "I live a few blocks from here, do you mind if we walk? So we have time to talk calmly."

"As you wish, just lead the way." I say

We walked toward her house. "Well, as you can imagine, it was not easy to overcome what happened to me that night. I had difficult days, I was depressed and fearful and I even thought of killing myself on few occasions. Luckily, my mother was always around to help me. She was always there to help me and support me.

She took me to a support group for women who were victims of rape and abuse. I learned a lot from those talks and I certainly became a stronger person and eventually I was able to overcome everything.

I went to the hospital where we were admitted. I wanted to know your whereabouts; to thank you for helping me out. I'm sure that without your timely intervention, I would have been killed. I was told that you have been discharged and I wasn't given any information on you.

My mother decided that we move elsewhere to steer me away from the memory of what happened at that park. She sold our house and bought another on this side of town. I wanted to look for you but I didn't know how and where exactly. And to be honest, I was really scared to go back to that place. I thank God every day for having put in my life and I asked that our paths meet again. Today my prayers were answered."

Silvia's words penetrated me deeply. Oh God, if she only knew that I was one of her rapists! It was tough knowing she thought I deserved to be called a hero and that on top of that she prayed for me.

It is true that I had changed since that night, but it didn't change the fact that I did what I did. I needed to figure out a way to tell her the truth, because it was not fair that she had a misconception of me.

Just as I thought I had found the words to begin my confession with regards to what happened that night, she says, "we're here. This is where I live. Please do come in." Taking a key from her handbag, she opened the door.

"Thank you," I replied. "I hope I'm not disturbing anyone."

"Don't worry; I just live here with my mother and my son…"

As she said it, a 5 year old boy went out to reach her. She ran to him and gave him a hug.

"Mommy, who is he?" The kid asked.

"He is a friend, my love. His name is Sergio, like you." She replied.

And she whispered into my ear,

"The only thing that people at the hospital told me is that your name is Sergio. So in honor, I named my child after you. I understand that he is not to blame for everything that happened and he's actually my reason for living."

Little Sergio came to greet me, looked me in the eyes intently. My God, that look, those olive eyes, that mole on the eyebrow. Sergio is the spitting image of my father!

How can I ever tell Silvia the truth? How do I tell Silvia that little Sergio is my son?

To think that she considers me a hero…

ALX

I checked myself out to make sure every detail on my outfit was perfect, it was important that I didn't miss a thing. After all this was going to be my first live performance and I was nervous!

I adjusted my hat, made sure that my shirt was tucked in and adjusted my coat. The boots were the perfect complement to the outfit. Image is very important in the show business. Although I don't consider myself someone who's vain I need to take care of my image because it goes hand-in-hand with my talent.

I looked at my image of Christ and said a quick prayer, I asked him to give me the strength to go out onto that stage and give it my all.

As I approach the stage I felt more nervous but also a thrill, because I was finally going to give a concert. I Wheaties three singles from my first album which were quickly placed on the top of charts. My manager begin looking for other places in which I could perform, this was one of the ones he chose. I hear the announcers voice, "there are many artist out there, but not many like him. His songs have topped the charts, his voice tingles the senses, he is a man who came to stay. Ladies and gentlemen directly from Mexicali Baja California he is…ALEX VILLARRAL!!!"

I can hear my name echoing throughout the arena.

Your man is here, the one that you've been waiting for

The one that only in dreams you imagined
Your man is finally here, come give me your hand
I want to hear you say it, I only love you

The lights travel all around the stage, people start clapping and chanting my name,

"ALEX…ALEX…ALEX"

I ask God for the strength again as I walk to the stage and I say to myself, "okay Alex it's time to give this stage the best you've got. You've long for this moment and it's finally here."

I want the people who have paid to see this concert to leave satisfied and glad to have come and see my performance.

Memories start flooding in. There were many people who didn't believe in me at first, who doubted my talents and my commitment to music. On more than one occasion I was told that I should focus on something else, because in the world of entertainment there was no room for me. My mother was always supportive of me though. Her words are deeply engraved in my mind and in my heart.

"Alejandro, do what you love most!"

What I love most is to sing. That's why am here.

I knew I had to fight to do what I love, because to me there is nothing that will fill me with more satisfaction then seeing people get excited about my music, My songs. Because only by doing what you love are you able to be you!

I hear the audience chanting for me to come out. I hear the sound of the band playing, it gets louder and louder. I finally come out and stand before the audience to greet them. Their shouts shaken me, I feel the love of the people and I can't help but smile. I lean toward them I take my head off as a greeting and say, "good evening and welcome! Thank you so much for being here on my very first concert. How many think I should start off with my latest single?"

I start to sing...

WANTED

I wanted to draw you as Leonardo drew his Mona Lisa
Not realizing how false your smile was
I devoted so much time to focusing on your features
The minutes I spent without you, felt so much longer

I wanted you to be the princess in my fairytales
But you pawned to always be the wicked witch
You changed the ending of the classic love story
To be one worthy of the greatest or movie

I want to make you the Juliet for that dreamer that was Romeo
You know? For you I would've died because of love and desire
Yet you treated me with arrogance and disdain
And whenever you could, you'd have me kneeling before your feet

I wanted you to be my guide, as Dante was for Beatrice
But by following in you I was made the happiest man
Because instead of taking my hand and taking me to heaven
You sent me to Hell, the man who loves you like no one else

I wanted you to be the start to each of my phrases
But you just pushed me to the side in the most cruel and macabre way
I wanted to give you my all but you did not care for it
Because your soul was poisoned and your heart rotten

As soon as I finish singing I hear Ismael, my roommate.

"Alejandro, Alejandro, Alejandro…wake up!"

"Damn it Alejandro, you've been singing at the top of your lungs for a while it's 4 in the morning!!"

"Sorry Ismael, I thought I was singing at a concert" I say confused

"Yeah, I imagined." He replies

"You just wait and see, Ismael. I'm going to make my dreams come true. Pretty soon, people will know and dance my music! Don't you forget it!" I say confidently

OH, MY AUGUSTINE!

The cold winter helped to make sense of the outfit I wore. I fixed my glasses, make sure my fake mustache is straight, put on my long coat, my hat and my scarf. I take a deep breath, get out of my car and walk into the library which was full to the maximum capacity.

I saw people reading, several were in groups. From time to time they would turn around to see if the author of the novel was walking through the door. "Oh My Augustine!" Is all anyone talked about.

I honestly did not expect my first novel to reach the record sells it did. It is not very common for an unknown writer to jump to fame so quickly after having published his first book, and even more rare that the public would ask for a book signing.

But there I was in the library in which I agreed to hold my first book signing. Since I had no experience in these sorts of things and not knowing how many people would attend the signing, I decided to arrive an hour early to prepare myself and watch the people would be there.

Inside the library was a café where people read while they enjoyed a coffee or a cup of hot chocolate and maybe some fruits.

My representative told me that the book was being talked about everywhere. The inconclusive love story won the hearts of the readers and it was inevitable for them still recommending it amongst friends, quickly making it popular.

What no one knew is that "Oh My Augustine!" was much more than just a simple unfinished love story. It was published on August 28 at my request, but it is a story which I had heard since I was just a child, the story that I grew up with.

I walked through the library watching the readers. There was people of all ages. I felt a mixture of pride and excitement to see that everyone had my novel in their hands. I walk into the cafeteria and see a group of people holding my book as they look eagerly at the door waiting to see the entrance of the author, ignorant to the fact that the author was actually looking at them.

A reader caught my attention. The man must have been in his mid 40s. Like me he was wearing glasses, he had long hair and a scarf on his head which made him look like a gypsy. He chose and a table for two at the back of the café, he looked down as he read my novel and I could see him bring up a silk scarf to dab his eyes. His face was too familiar, but I know I had never seen him before.

I couldn't help but approach them and ask, "excuse me sir, do you mind if I sit here? There are too many people and I'd like to be away from the others."

He looked up at me and said, "of course young man, have a seat."

"Thank you, you're very kind." I replied. "Do you like the novel?"

"Of course it practically describes my life! This really is my life story. I'm here because I want to meet the author and see if I could have the opportunity to talk to him and ask him who told him the story." He says.

"Are you sure?" I ask, now I'm fully interested.

"Yes, my name is Augustine Lopez and although the novel did not mention my name. I know that it is talking about me." He says as he pulls out his ID.

I observe him carefully, and indeed his age and physical attributes coincide with the Augustine described in my novel, but it cannot be true. Augustine had already died.

"Could you tell me why Natalia believed him to be dead? In the novel Augustine died." I say

He explained, "Natalia and I love each other since we were kids. We went to the same school, she was my first girlfriend and I was her first boyfriend. We were seeing each other secretly because her father did not approve our relationship, being as my family was poor. I'm sure you knew that part because it is written in the novel. When we turned 20 years old we decided that we would get married despite what anyone said. We planned on running away to the City of Mexico to start a new life there. We were planning on moving on August 28, 1962, because that was the date of our anniversary as lovers. With a lot of effort, we managed to save enough money and we bought bus tickets. I waited at the bus terminal, the last bus was to leave at 7 PM. I arrived an hour early and anxiously waited for her. I waited an hour then two then three and she never showed up.

As I walked home, I was jumped and mugged. The little bit of money I had saved up was stolen. When I woke up, I was in a small town hospital. I was told that I was found lying on the roadside in Sonora.

Sonora? I didn't know anyone there. I lived in Guanajuato my whole life and was never far away from my family. I was penniless and in the hospital in which I had to stay in for a few days. I had to work hard to be able to pay my dues at the hospital. I rented a place, and worked hard and save money to return to Guanajuato.

In total I stayed in Sonora for about five months. Five months that seem like an eternity. When I finally was able to pay everything that I owed to the hospital I saved up for my ticket back to Guanajuato and some extra money for unexpected expenditures.

I came home to my parents. After the initial shock of seeing me, they told me that I had been presumed dead. People rumored how I had been mugged and murdered and that my body had disappeared. That was in the worst part though, I received the painful news that Natalia married another man and moved away to live with him.

I looked for her in many places but it was like trying to find a needlestick in a hey sack. I painfully decided that if she wanted to see me, she would've already reached out to me."

"She never cared to look because just like everyone else, she thought you were dead." I said

"How do you know that? Did you know her? If so, please tell me where I can find her. I need to see her at once!"

"Do you still love her? It's been 25 years since."

"Do I still love her? I never stopped loving her!!!"

With that being said, he opens his briefcase and pulls out a photo showing the Natalia and him. Both were very young, hugging and happy, you could see the immense love they have for each other. I took the picture and stroked it with my thumb.

I take my glasses off along with the fake mustache and say, "I'm a Augusto Bautista, the author of the book. Natalia was forced to marry another man because the afternoon that you both agreed to in the open she fainted. Her parents took her to the hospital and found out that she was pregnant. She told her parents that you needed to be informed that you were going to be a father and that you guys were to be married soon. Her father said that he would bring you to her. But because he disapproved after she told him of your meeting place he ordered the assault.

After that he told Natalia that you had been murdered. A victim of robbers. They arrange for her to be married with another man, then they went to live in Chiapas. No one said anything to prevent the people of the town for learning that she had been pregnant.

Natalia gave birth to a boy, and although she couldn't give him the last name of his biological father, she gave him the same first name."

"Where is Natalia?" Augustine asked with tears in his eyes. "Please, I need to see her"

"She died a little over a year ago, on August 28 she died in my arms. So I wanted to write her story because she never stopped loving Augustine. For me, it was the best way to pay tribute to the woman I love most in the world. The woman who always hugged me and told me sighing, "oh my Augustine!"

"Are you saying…?"

"YES DADDY. I AM NATALIA'S SON!!!"

WITNESS

My father always told me, "Mauricio, do not look at what does not concern you. If by chance you see something that you shouldn't, be cautious to get away as soon as possible without anyone seeing you. It may cost you dearly."

He wasn't lying…

I was at a party with some friends, celebrating that our favorite soccer team won the championship game after so many years of losing. It was also our last day of vacation before going back to college.

We were there for a hours drinking as of the world was coming to an end. I got up to go to the restroom for the umpteenth time as I pass by the bartender I said, "I'd like to settle the bill, my friends and I can't drink anymore otherwise we'll explode." I handed him my card and told him I would be back.

After relieving myself I grab my card and head back to the table were my friends were still consuming the buckets of beer.

"Mauricio, I just bet Juan and Miguel that you're still good to drink three beers back to back" Gerardo says.

"Just 3?" I reply "I can drink 10!"

"I don't think so. It's easier said than done" Miguel says.

Determined to prove them wrong I grab the bottle of beer and start drinking. I lost count after a few. Next thing I know I'm being woken up by the bartender, "hey we're closing. You want me to call a taxi?"

I thought he was joking but when I turned and looked around, I saw no one…except him and myself.

"Where are my friends?" I asked confused

"The bailed roughly 2 hours ago. They tried to wake you but you wouldn't budge, so they decided to leave without you but not without assuring me you would be alright once you took a nap."

"Thank you" I reply. "It's alright, you told to call a taxi for me I live within walking distance. I rather work so I can shake off whatever effect is left from the beer."

I had been walking about 10 minutes when I felt the urge to pee. The beers I consumed surely took it's toll on me. I turned into a nearby alley to discreetly relieve myself. I have been caught once before and had to pay a hefty amount to a cop so he wouldn't take me in. I began to empty my bladder when I heard a strange noise. I rushed to finish and ducked near one of the large dumpsters. I put my hands inside my pockets to check and see if I have anything of value. I pull out my wallet and drop it on the ground nearby just in case it was a thief. I was thinking of how I'd return to retrieve it early in the morning when I saw him.

He was a tall, burly guy. He was carrying something on his shoulders and came pretty close to the spot where I was hiding when he dropped his load. As it hit the ground I heard a moan. Heavens! The guy was carrying a woman and he'd just dropped her. He took off his clothes and began to rape her. My heart was pounding so hard that I feared he'd hear it.

The effects of the alcohol wore off instantly. I was thinking of how I could get out of there when I saw a light coming down the alley. The guy gets up hides behind a wall. It was a cop doing his rounds in the area. He might've heard the noise and came to investigate. When he saw the woman on the floor he ran to help her. The guy takes this opportunity to attack the policeman. Giving him a sharp blow to the head which knocked him out, the lit flashlight falls and allowed me to see the guy pull out a knife and plunge it repeatedly into the body of the policeman. I also managed to see that the guy had a tattoo of the tiger on his right arm. He takes a flashlight turns it off and continues to violate the girl. Taking advantage that his back was turned to me I make a run for it.

I ran the whole way home, but got very little sleep that night. Any little noise startled me, I constantly peaked out my window fearing I'd see the guy outside the house waiting for me. The night seemed eternal and I couldn't shake the thought from my head, had I been more modest and not drank so much I would have left the bar with my friends and wouldn't have had to witness such a terrible crime.

The next day, I shower and get ready to go to college. I'd be meeting new classmates and you teachers, maybe that would help me relax and get my mind off of things. I contemplated whether I should make a report to the police about what happened in the alley.

I was thinking about what happened the night before when I entered my classroom, the professor was already there, his back facing me. He was tall and stocky, I quickly took a seat.

When the teacher turned around our eyes meet. I smile and he smiles back, his smile was the most enigmatic and mocking one I had ever seen.

He reaches into his briefcase, and pulls out my wallet. Smiling he says, "Good morning Mauricio. Judging by the look on your face you haven't slept well."

As he extends his arm to hand me my wallet his sleeve slides up his arm revealing a tiger tattoo, the one I saw last night.

PROCESSION

Never have I seen so many people in my life, I One dude what's happening.

They all looked at me with curiosity. They're not familiar faces but they look at me as if they've known me my whole life.

Some, very few, are friends of mine

Since my name has become more well known, many people try to get close to me to use me.

My father, a small time actor, always told me, "Gamaliel, the more famous you are the more people will seek you. This is why I am happy in my small town theater because my friends know me and would not give me their back. You, you want to be a big time actor and you want to go international. You must understand that fame comes with a high price."

I soon realized that those words were very true.

For sometime, I had been in love with Karina, a woman who for almost 4 years evaded me. However after my first film, "Run!", was nominated and won best film of the year, Karina was the one to ask me out.

I couldn't be happier. Not only did my debut film prove to be a blockbuster movie, it was also nominated and won at the film festival. On top of that, the woman who I've always liked had now become my girlfriend. I was meeting a lot of important people and had many friends.

After my film was shown everywhere the offers started flying in. Movie producers were now fighting with each other to have me in their films. I felt like I was on top of the world. The film shootings were done in various parts of the world. This left me with very little time to see my father. I was absorbed completely in this world, I couldn't believe my life has change so drastically.

A few months into dating Karina, I came home to find her fooling around in bed with one of my best friends. Regardless of how much I loved her there was no time to get to depressed over her betrayal. Soon after the break up I met Veronica. She was a stunning woman and a budding celebrity. I met her through Julio, a friend.

Veronica and I were on the front pages of every major newspaper in the country. Everyone complimented me on how beautiful my new girlfriend was. She was part of a talk show, she was always proclaiming how much we loved each other, and announcing that we would be getting married. I simply kept quiet and let everyone believe that there was going to be a wedding.

My relationship with her also failed. This time it was the paparazzi who pointed out her betrayal. Photos of her and Julio circulated everywhere and left no doubt that they had a long-standing romance going on.

With the amount of scandal that followed my second break up. I decided to get away and pay my father a visit.

"Son, remember when I told you? Many people will approach you because you are a star." He said

"Can't they see me for who I am and not for what I have?"

"Unfortunately no, most people won't son. I warned you about this, before you decided you wanted to be a part of that world."

I spent all afternoon with him then went home, the next day I would be traveling to Milan, Italy to start shooting another film.

Seven years went by if you blink of an eye. I career was at its peak, I was highest paid actor. Contrary to how successful my career was, my love life was a failure. The media assumed any woman they saw me with publicly was my girlfriend or someone I was dating. Soon enough they gave me the reputation of being a "womanizer"

My father died in an accident, I was in Turkey in the middle of recording for a film at the time that it happened. I had a lot of trouble finding a last minute flight home so I could make it to his funeral in time.

Like with everything else, the media became aware and pushed for interviews. I asked that they at least respect my grief and they did.

I wasn't able to mourn for long, I was needed to return to Turkey to finish filming. I returned to work to demonstrate why I was the bus I'm terrible.

The final scenes of the film required my character to fall back from the third floor. As usual I did not want to use a stunt double. The scene did not seem dangerous, I just had to be careful in calculating my fall so I wouldn't fall outside the protective netting.

I closed my eyes as required by the shot, I thought of my father and I let myself fall…

"Gamaliel" I swear it was my father's voice "Gamaliel, come."

Then I hear Vincente, an old friend of mine, "Gamaliel, I still can't believe it. Why you?"

"Why?" Vicente said, hugging Diego.

"Vicente, I know it's difficult to except but we have to be strong." The Diego told him.

I don't understand what's happening. What are they talking about?

Vicente's eyes look down at me with deep sorrow and tears began to fall on my face.

"You're attention please." I do not recognize this voice "I'd like to ask everyone to please clear the area. We are going to start the funeral procession to dismiss a great actor, a man who showed his professionalism to the very end, a man who certainly leaves a huge void in the world of entertainment. Goodbye. Lets all stand and and give a warm round of applause to the great Christian Gamaliel Muñoz!"

A funeral procession? My funeral procession?

RUN!

"Bobby one day you will regret having purchased a cabin so far from the city" my father said to me when I informed him about that acquisition, today, those words resonate strongly within me.

My cabin is not only far from the city, it is also very close to the sharp curve where lots of car accidents occurred because of the high-speed people will drive at. For this reason I sleep in the living room a lot, so that in case of an emergency I hear it and go help someone.

Let's night at about 11 PM, I open one of the windows in the room, because of the weather and also to save energy. The window is covered with mosquito net, all the other windows in the cabin are tightly shut. There's also a back door that I leave open since it's not visible from the road.

I half heartedly watch an old Western movie on the television. I sought out an interesting program but found nothing so had to settle for this. I was laying on the couch with a bottle of whiskey resting on the table wen I decided to read instead.

I was about to take my second glass of whiskey on the rocks when they heard the noise…

The grinding of brakes was unmistakable, the screeching of the tires hurt my eardrums, I could only imagine what it did to the driver's. The smell of burning tires was strong and irritated my nose then I heard glass shatter. Despite not being able to see the actual scene, I could see the glass scattered everywhere.

"Well, let's see if there's any unfortunate victims." I said to myself

I stood up, Took a sip of whiskey straight from the bottle, put my sneakers on and left the cabin.

When I saw the car I ran as fast as I could and reached it in a few minutes. It was upside down, I saw young woman seated in the driver seat. Her for head hit the windshield and caused her to lose consciousness. The airbag was pierced with a piece of glass. The woman had a wound on her for head so I hastily pulled her out of the car. I saw her and bag and cell phone and grabbed it. We hadn't gotten far from the car when the car suddenly burst out in flames.

"God, that was close!"

I carried the woman and went to my cabin. I took her into my bedroom to attend her wound, she remained unconscious.

I watched her carefully, her black hair reached her mid back. She had brown skin and very black curly eyelashes, her nose complemented her face and lips. I wondered what color her eyes were. I determined that she was certainly a pretty woman. As of her nationality, I was unsure. She looked at Latina, but there was something different.

Once I finished with the first aide care, I called up my friend, Colton Kenneth Davidson. He was a medical intern and I wanted him to check on the woman to see if she needed to be admitted to a hospital. I didn't call an ambulance since I didn't want the police to get involved yet. I wasn't ready for all the questions, such as why didn't call the police sooner or why I had administered first aid to her myself. Frankly, something within me told me what I had done was the right thing.

"Colton" I said once he answers the phone call, "it's Bobby Moss. Yeah, I know it's Saturday and close to midnight. But I need you to do me a huge favor. Can you come to my home? I need you to check on a woman who just got into an accident."

Colton arrives a little after 15 minutes. He carefully examines the woman and says, "there's nothing serious worth worrying about, just a blow to her head. You did a good job in administering the first aid care. I'll leave some painkillers with you that she can take when she wakes up. I'll be back in the morning to check up on her."

"Thank you Colton, I owe you one. I'll wait for your return tomorrow. Come on, I'll see you to the door." I said extending him my hand

After Colts and leaves, I go back to the bedroom to check on the woman and found her sleeping peacefully. I returned to the living room and turn the television off. I put in an instrumental CD so that I can meditate. It would certainly be a serious problem should police find out that I housed a woman who got into a car accident. I could very well be arrested. I started to close all the windows turn off the lights, except the lamp on the nightstand table to illuminate the room. I poured myself another glass of whiskey and lean back on the couch. In the case the cops arrive, I will say that I did not hear anything because I was listening to music and drinking till I fell asleep.

Soon enough, I hear the sound of the ambulance and fire fighters. Certainly someone who just happened to be out there saw the car in flames and made the call.

Not five minutes had gone by when I heard the knock on my door. My, how quickly they have decided to come and ask about the accident.

I answer the door without opening it. "Yes, who's there?" I try to make my voice sound sleepy.

"Can I ask you some questions? I am Detective Marc Grandoni, may I come in?" A voice with his strong Italian accent asks.

I open the door thinking to myself, a detective? The police were supposed to be interrogating.

The detective shows me his identification. I take it, check his name, and compare the photo with his face. He had short curly hair, blue eyes, bushy eyebrows, and a straight nose, and thick lips. I return the identification card and asked how I may help him.

"I just thought that maybe because the accident happened not far from here…" He begins to say as he inspects the room with sharp eyes, which catch me by surprise. I didn't like his behavior at all so I immediately interrupt him, "actually, I just heard the ambulance and patrol cars passed by, I was having a couple of shots of whiskey earlier and fell asleep. Can I offer you something to drink?"

"That's very kind of you, I would greatly appreciated if I could have a glass of water." He responds

"Please take a seat" I said and went to the kitchen to finish his request. Immediately, I come back and give him the glass of water.

He accepts the drink appreciatively and drinks the contents, then he said, "did you really not hear or see anything?" He asked again, he looked straight into my eyes. "I'm asking you because the person who was driving the vehicle is a very dangerous woman. She's a ruthless killer and was among one of the most wanted by the CIA and FBI. If she survived the accident she should be around here somewhere. I'm urging you to be careful and use extreme security measures and if you see her report it to me right away."

With that said, he hands me a card with his name and cell phone number on it. Then we both saw two silhouettes of policemen who were heading towards my cabin.

"I must go, don't forget what I just told." He says he hurried to the door and within seconds was no where to be seen.

I had not even close the door when someone knocked on it again this time it was the police. I told them the same thing that I told the detective. I had been drinking while listening to music loudly and fell asleep. I was awaken by the noise of the ambulance and patrol cars passing by, only then did I realized that an accident occurred.

"Perhaps there wasn't only one car. Maybe there were two cars and one overturned. The other driver pulled out of the one in the accident and drove away. Tomorrow we'll find out who rented that vehicle. Being as the license plate indicates it's a rental." Says one of the cops.

They left and I was left more confused than ever. First the detective tells me that the woman who was sleeping in my bedroom was a killer and now the police say the car was rented.

I decided to going to the bedroom to check on the woman and found her sleeping peacefully still. Looking at her and I couldn't imagine the detectives words to be true. She didn't look like a killer, her features were those of a very beautiful woman. It's not to say that a murderer has a specific type of appearance, but something in me refused to believe what the detective said. I search the bag I found in the car and find her ID, Leanna Dassrath, born in Trinidad. Now it made sense as to why she looked Latina. Amongst the usual things if I'm in the woman's purse I found a card from the club in the front it said "Dubai", on the back with the note, "full service, absolute discretion" and number.

Woman as beautiful as she was going to places like those? Questions rushed through my head, then I saw the flashing light from the cell phone. It dawned on me I hadn't notified any relatives of hers. I was about to pick it up when I realized that the number on the caller ID asked the number on the card I had just found.

I decided not to pick up and let it vibrate hoping whoever was calling would give up. I went to the living room, ready to sleep, there would be time to clarify everything with this woman tomorrow morning.

At about 7 AM I woke up on the couch where I fell asleep. I walk into the bedroom to find that the woman has already awakened and is sitting on the edge of the bed. As I enter the room she asks, "who are you and how did I end up here?"

"Calm down, I will explain. My name is Bobby Moss, last night you were in an accident and I brought you here. While you were unconscious, I asked a friend of mine to come over and check you out. He said you were fine."

"I need to go" she says standing up. "No, don't. You still need to be examined by my friend. You're safe here." I protested

"I really need to go, otherwise I can put you at risk"

"I'm sorry?" I asked confused "you really don't have to. The injury you sustained from the accident wasn't that serious but you need to rest sit down and I'll prepare breakfast for you"

She repeats again, "I really need to go, you can't tell anybody that I've been here, it's for your own good."

"Why don't you just tell me what the problem is? Believe me, I will help you however I can"

"I'll check I need to be as brief as possible" she said as she says as she sits on the couch. "A month ago, I was going to marry my boyfriend. The day of the wedding came and he never showed up. I went into a deep depression and wanted to take my own life, but I couldn't bring myself to doing it. So I searched several websites for hitmen services and came across a club named Dubai. I was told they're the best, fast and never fail. I paid the amount they were asking and gave them my information. This was a week ago, but the day after I did that I found out that my fiancee did not show up to the wedding because he was kidnapped and murdered not because he was a coward like I thought him to be. I talked to the agency to tell them I no longer wanted them to move along with the teal, but they said that they do not accept cancellations after a contract has been made."

"Do you know the name of the assassin?" I asked, when I see a red light shining with in my night lamp.

"I was told his name was Marco Grandoni..."

I gesture her to keep quiet with my finger over my lips. The red light within my night lamp has stopped shining. That light shouldn't be there, my phone lights up, I see it's a message from my friend Colton:

"I was about to go to your house when I saw a guy standing outside, he has a gun! I called the police. They said they'll be here soon!"

I hear a knock on the door, I take the woman's hand, pulled her towards the back door and say, "RUN!"

EL CACHITO
(THE LOTTERY TICKET)

With tears in my eyes cut the ribbon, I was officially opening the support center for lost and exploited children called, El Cachito.

I want the whole thing to be something very intimate. A small ceremony in which only a few close friends, the staff, the lawyer and priest who helped get everything together would attend. However, it was inevitable that the press find out and so there they were, radio reporters, television reporters with their cameramen, and journalists who arrived very early to send their notes to the editorials.

El Cachito. People questioned how I came up with such a name for the organization. More so, they wondered why such a successful entrepreneur as myself was even interested in establishing this organization free of charge to anyone especially since I didn't have the support of other entrepreneurs.

As I'm cutting the ribbon, I close my eyes for a moment and the memories flood my mind.

"Please sir won't you buy just one ticket, I haven't sold one today and you'll probably get lucky" I heard his voice say

I was walking out of the Basilica of Lady Guadalupe. I had come to pray for my wife as I did each year.

I was hungry and saw a man selling tacos across the street. The little kid approached me once I crossed the street. His jeans were worn down, his shirt so dirty it was impossible to make out the color, his shoes were so old and torn that both his feet were exposed. His face and hands were clean though.

It broke my heart to see him like this. It was already 6 PM and if he really hasn't sold anything all day, it was safe to assume that he must be hungry.

"Come, let's eat some tacos and then I'll buy some tickets" I say to him.

"Really?!?!" His face lights up "thank you sir!"

He devoured the tacos. I bought 10 tickets because that's all I had enough for. He thanked me and hurried off saying he had to continue selling more tickets.

I couldn't shake the image of his face in the days that followed. So when one of the scratch offs turned out to be quite the winning I made it my mission to find him so I could compensate him. I'd always live comfortably but now I was very wealthy and didn't have to worry about my financial future. It wouldn't be an easy task, I'd have to dedicate a lot of time to walking through the city streets looking for him.

I found him a few days later, he was near a taco stand. I observed him for a little while I could see the hunger in his eyes, I approach him slowly and I felt a strange sensation in my heart, something I don't know how to explain. I tapped him on the shoulder and he quickly turned around with a frightened look on his face.

"Don't be frightened, I just want to thank you for the luck that you gave me with those scratch off tickets you sold me the other day, you said that I'd get lucky and sure enough I did so I came to give you a gift"

I placed a few bills in his palm. He looks at them eyes bulged open. Then he asked, "Are they all for me?" I saw him look across the street with frightened eyes. He looks at me and says, "I must go thank you so much sir." He rushes across the street.

It all happened so quickly. The impact was so hard it flung his little body up high. The driver took off before anyone could take a look at his license plate. I looked up towards where the boy was looking and saw who was without a doubt the man exploiting him. He looked rugged and mean, he stared at the bloody body then ran.

I ran to the boys side, by the time the ambulance got there it was too late.

He'd already pass.

As I looked down at him I saw something that crushed my heart and tore my soul. His shirt was pulled up and a mole on his chest was exposed. It was identical to the one my wife had. My wife who passed away, not being able to bear the loss of our son who was stolen when he was only 2 years old.

VIRGEN FOR SALE

"Mary…Mary…are you paying attention to me?"

"Sorry Lucy…what were you saying?"

"What are you thinking about? I was telling you that all the catechist are getting together at Teresa's house. Her mom wants us to help decorate the house. Her eldest son gets home from Mexico City. Can you believe that he's already a lawyer? I heard he's very handsome and Teresa has told him a lot about you."

"Lucy, I'm sorry but I'm not going to be able to go because…"

"But your parents are away! Come on, it's been a while since you've hung out with us"

"Trust me I'd love to. I really can't though, my aunt is ill and I should go visit her since my parents are away. She lives a bit far so I need to leave early."

"Oh ok. I understand. If you'd like I can accompany you."

"No, don't worry about it. Teresa would be upset if not only one but 2 of her friends didn't show. Tell her I'm sorry."

"Alright please be safe. I'll see you tomorrow."

Finally she leaves me alone, I can't stand her! I need to hurry. I still have to get my wardrobe completely ready. I have to sew up the vail, the guy last week tore. There's no doubt that there's something about the idea of having a virgin that's drives men crazy. Such fools.

Well here I am again. The place always looks the same: dimly lit, there's furniture and decorations that give this place the homie feel. It's all set up to cover up what really goes on. The owner, of course, is very cautious when selecting the clientele. Only very wealthy men can afford to be here. I wonder how much he charges them. Oh well it doesn't matter, he pays me well, besides some of the men I'm with give me more money.

"Ready Mary?" Madame Leonora asks, she's in charge of catering to the clients while they decide which girl they want.

"Of course Leonora, who wants to be with the Virgin Mary tonight?"

"It was such a clever idea to dress up as the VIrgin Mary. Every time you come there's more and more men who ask to be with you. You've become quite the sensation. But only you can pull the look off, with your delicate brown skin, beautiful innocent appearance."

"Thank you, let's get going or he might get impatient"

I got lucky tonight. The man who paid to be with me is young, can't be older than 30. He's muscular and handsome. Judging by his clothes he has a lot of money. I'll definitely enjoy myself tonight. I'm going to blow his mind, maybe he'll leave extra money.

Whew! What a night! He was an amazing lover, to bad he didn't even say bye. I'll probably never see him again. I usually don't have repetitive customers.

I was getting ready to walk out the bedroom when I saw the note:

"Thank you for such a pleasurable evening. You are very skilled in bed. I picked you because you look a lot like a friend of my sister's. I'm supposed to meet her tonight at my mothers house. Your resemblance is strictly physical, being as she's a catechist and you a prostitute."

THE WRITER

The phone doesn't stop ringing. Clearly whoever it is must really want to talk to me, this is the 5th time they call. Who could it be? I avoid using my phone while driving. I've seen it cause to many tragic accidents, and I've never felt it's worth the risk.

Just when I think they've given up, I hear the phone ring again. I'll answer but I'll be brief.

"Hello?" I say not so pleasantly.

"Salvador! Hey! Thank goodness you answer. It's Orlando Mediola" Your editor.

"Hi. Sorry I'm driving. What can I do for you?"

"Listen to this! I got a phone call from a production company that wants to make a film out of your novel, "Black Rose." Quite frankly that scene in which the girl is sinking and the guy comes in with nothing but a rope is pretty intense. I thought he was going to choke her."

"Wait…did you just say he saves her? In my novel he chokes her!"

"Salvador stop messing around, I have the book in my hands. I know what I'm talking about"

"Orlando, I'm not kidding" I say frustrated "I don't normally keep a copy of what I write at home but I know very well what I write. I've never written out a scene like the one you're describing"

"Look Salvador, there's has to be some kind of misunderstanding. As soon as you can go over what you wrote and get back to me. I don't want to distract you any longer while you drive."

"Alright, but I know for sure this is a mistake."

The drive home seems eternal. Ricardo Cano will hear my mouth! He's the one to blame for this mistake, he corrects and edits my writings.

I'm so focused on what I'm going to tell Ricardo that I almost hit a man!

I quickly hit the brakes and my tires screech. The guy is dressed in black. He's wearing a trench coat with a high collar and black hat. I came so close to hitting him but he seems unfazed, he slowly turns to look at me, I see a sparkle in his eyes.

"Watch where you're going!" I yell.

He stares at me for a few seconds and I think he mumbled something while mockingly smiling. He turns back around and continues to walk slowly as if nothing happened.

"Suicidal prick!" I yell. He seemed to be deaf because he didn't turn around, simply continued walking. I drive off and when I look in my rear view mirror, I no longer see him. But I know it wasn't a figment of my imagination.

As soon as I get home, to my cabin, I head straight for my office. I keep copies of the drafts of my books there. I find

"Black Rose", I take it and head to the living room. I light up the fireplace since it's starting to cool down. Grab a glass and pour some whiskey from my mini bar, I chug the first glass. As I'm about to pour myself another drink I hear something. I try to fixate my ears on the sound, but suddenly everything is silent.

I forget about the noise and focus on my novel. I flip to the end and sure enough The swamp scene is just as I remember writing it...

Rosa walks blindly without realizing that she's moving into the swamp. She suddenly feels something wet underneath her feet, she tries to walk backwards but she's already sinking. She panics, and then holds still remembering that it'd keep her from sinking as quickly. She yells and sees Ulises walking towards her. She forgets about their argument. He throws a rope at her to put around her body. He throws herself at him, that's when he ties a second rope around her neck. Pulls and snaps it. He cuts both ropes and let's her body sink.

I knew it! Who does Ricardo think he is, changing what I wrote. I'm frustrated and pick up the phone to call him.

"Hello? This is Ricardo Cano. How may I help you?"

"Ricardo, it's Salvador Morales Villalobos. Who the heck authorized you to change my story?!?!"

"Calm down Salvador, looks I've always believed you're very talented. But frankly your endings are pathetic."

"Is that what you think of me? Why'd you accept to work with me?"

"Because I believe in you. You've got talent, you write great stories, it's just your endings aren't believable. I have a lot of experience in the world of literate. I know what sells and what doesn't. If I didn't change the endings to your stories, they wouldn't be as successful…"

I interrupt, "the endings you give them? You mean to tell me this isn't the only book you've done it to?"

"Salvador, please listen to me. I'm the expert in selling stuff here. Rather than being upset with me I think you should be thanking me. I helped make Faceless Woman, Suicidal Souls, The Other Face of the Mirror, and The Good Son into hits and you the writer of the decade."

"What makes you think that's what I want? I just want my books to be published, as I write them. I don't care if whether they're a hit or not!"

"Look Salvador, in the world literature us editors have to make sure that what is being published is not a waste of money. If all you care about is being happy with yourself, I suggest you self publish your books. Honestly I don't think the ending to your latest novel The Writer is a good one as well. Who believes in appearances on the road? Who's going to want to read your story about a writer who almost hits a man on his way to his cabin, who suddenly disappears out of no where. A writer who in the end mysteriously dies after a telephone discussion with his editor. Not even a child could be forced to."

I hang up on him. I hear that sound outside again. It sounds as if someone is tiptoeing. I see a shadow, when I freeze. I hadn't realized that the events that had taken place on that evening were coinciding with those in my latest novel.

The writer also bears my name, he also has an argument with his editor. He hears strange sounds outside his cabin. He is stabbed and dies after he peeks outside to see what the shadow is…

As I am doing now.

MEMORY

I had transferred all the photos on my laptop to a USB drive. I was in my car and decided to get off to take pictures of our city's Capitol. I wanted to try out my cell phone camera. Being as its was equipped with the latest technology.

I put the USB drive in my pocket as I get off. At that time at night the Capitol building is deserted. It looked so majestic. The building was surrounded with big bronze sculptures. I began taking pictures of the sculptures. The camera worked marvelous.

Towards The back of the building there's a fountain with a centaur in the center and two angels to the side. Lights shine directly on the centaur the water comes out through his mouth and it gives the impression of being colorful. I take some pictures then head over to another sculpture of three men who are the founders of the states. Behind the statues is the river.

After a few more photos I sit down on the bench to look over the pictures I've taken so I can decide which ones I'd keep and which ones I'd delete.

I looked down at my watch and see that it is 11:30 PM. I was supposed to meet with some friends at a bar. I was about to grab my phone to call them and tell them that I got caught up taking pictures here, when I hear the a ring. It wasn't my phone, I look to the left that's where the ringing was coming from. I see the phone light up and I grab it to answer it, thinking that it must be the owner calling, to see where he forgot it. Before I can say a word I hear:

"Listen here you prick! We have your girl and we will kill her without hesitation if you don't do what we ask. Pay close attention and don't interrupt me, we will be waiting for you in 15 minutes at the entrance of the bar on Main Street, bring the memory stick you stole from us. More importantly don't tell anyone or you will not live to tell about it, understood?"

Without letting me say a word the guy hangs up. They called from a private number. I go through the contact list to see if I can find someone to call but it's empty. As if the cell phone had recently been purchased. The guy I spoke to clearly knows the number and the owner though. I get in my car and head to the bar that I was told to go to, I'm hoping they'll be a lot of people outside and that's this will keep them from hurting the girl.

I park and get off I'll block away from the bar, and I start walking. I want to see them from a distance. I'm only a few steps away from the bar when the phone rings again. Crap, I should've put it on vibrate! They hear the phone ring and my cover is blown, I see one guy hug the girl she's clearly frightened. The other guy shows me a gun inside his jacket and motions me to stop walking.

I answer and he says, "we cannot go through with the exchange here, there's too many witnesses. Meet us in 15 minutes at the central cabin in St. Joseph's park."

He hangs up and they walk away with the girl. Once they are out of my sight I walk back to the car. The phone rings for the third time. This time a number shows up on the caller ID. I answer and before they can say a word I begin to explain, "my name is Josh Kaplan, I accidentally found this phone a few minutes ago on a bench outside the Capitol. Some guys called this phone saying that they have a girl and they need some memory stick in exchange for her life. Do you know the owner of this phone?"

"Hold on I will transfer you to someone else" the voice sounds a bit familiar but I can't think of who it is.

The another woman talks, "hi, I'm attentive and we are aware of the situation. The memory drive they are talking about contains sensitive information. It is of great importance that this memory drive doesn't fall in their hands, what did he tell you?"

I tell her what they told me and she tells me to go to the place where I was told to meet them. That they would be sending in some help. That'd they'd get the girl and me out of there safely ones they had to the situation under control.

Feeling a little more calm I drive to the park and leave my car at the entrance. I walk to the cabin and I see the two guys with the girl. One of them asked for the USB, I pull out the one I had in my pocket with the pictures and show it to them. I tell him that I will only hand it to them once they let the girl get away from them. After that I hear that voice again behind me, the one on the phone who transferred me to the detective. I immediately recognize it, I've heard the voice many times before, we've shared many things together.

"I'm not sure how this memory stick came to be in your hands Josh and I'm really sorry, but we can't risk leaving any witnesses."

I turn immediately to look at my best friend!

Before I could explain that they were making a mistake, and before I could tell them that this USB drive only had pictures, I see my friends and on a gun with a silencer. He is approaching quickly. With his free hand he takes the memory stick and points the gun to my head. He says to the others, "kill her, I'll take care of him."

Last thing I feel is the impact on my head. Then I hear nothing else, I feel nothing else.

UNTIL I WANT TO

"Leonardo? Leonardo are you ok?" Aranzazu says

As soon as she walked in I recognized her. Ariella Kaplan.

We were having dinner at the best restaurant in Los Angeles, three years ago I decided to travel to the United States and go international. I was with my wife, Aranzazu, my manager Gerald Richardson, (His nick name is GL) and his girlfriend Kate Fallon.

There was a lot to celebrate. That morning GL called me to say that I was given the lead role in the new version of the movie, "Temptations of Jesus." By midday my wife came home singing of joy because her doctor confirmed that we were going to be parents. We had been married five years and we hadn't been able to get pregnant, so I immediately called GL and told him, "we must have dinner at the best restaurant. We have to celebrate big time, because not only did I get the role of Jesus, I'm also going to be a dad!"

At 4 PM, I received a phone call from the president of one of the TV stations and Mexico. He told me that the votes were in and that my soap opera, The Face of Good and Evil" had just won the Soap Opera of the Year Award and that next Saturday I would be their Guest of honor. A first class flight was booked already for me and it was important that I be there. Not only to be presented with the award but also to be given recognition for my great career as an actor.

As an actor I had accomplished a lot, as a singer not so much.

In my 15 years of work, I received award after award, complement after complement. An award for best male actor, best villain, best movie, best soap opera, etc.

I wanted more, Leonardo Falcon needed to be remembered as the greatest international star that ever lived!

It wasn't enough to receive so much recognition for being such a great actor, I also wanted to be known as a great singer. People didn't understand my musical concept, They weren't ready for it. My first album wasn't the hit I wanted it to be, the radio stations didn't support me the same way TV stations did. I'm sure has they played my music on the radio more often my first album would've been a bestseller.

To fund my second album I had to pull a lot of strings with my television connections. It was the best album that would be presented in Mexico. Everything was impeccable, the lyrics very original, it was totally unconventional. I was sure the audience was in for quite a surprise, but again no sales generated.

I decided to put off music for a while, just for a while.

As if all the good news I received the day wasn't enough; I received a phone call from my representative in United States, Fabian Vallejo.

"Leonardo, what projects do you have coming up?"he asks gleefully

"Hi Fabian, this morning he spoke with GL and he informed me that I got the lead role in Temptations of Jesus" I say

"I'm going to need you to only work on that Monday through Wednesday, I just got you the role as Judas in the play "I Judas." The functions will be from Thursday to Sunday and there will be at least 500 performances. Can you imagine that? You'll be playing Judas in the theater and Jesus in a film. This will be great for your career you will be unstoppable!"

"Oh man! Today is definitely the best day of my life! I've come so far" I say happily.

Once again I call GL and say, "GL there's a lot to celebrate today! So look for the best restaurant and make sure that will be no paparazzi tonight I want it to just be the four of us."

We arrived at the restaurant, which was indeed luxurious. It was reputed to be the most frequented restaurant by famous personalities. It was the most expensive, it's dishes were exquisite an exclusive. Most importantly, it was very difficult for any reporters to get in.

That's why I was surprised when I saw her walk in.

She walked in elegantly and confidently, like a black panther. She was just completely in black, her sharp intense and intelligent gaze met my eyes briefly, then she turned to see my companions, after looking back at me again. The memory of her last interview with me came back into my mind and I was filled with rage.

It was two weeks ago that she had interviewed me unexpectedly. I didn't expect to see her for a long time, no reporter had ever made me feel like such an imbecile. Not satisfied with that she had audacity to air our interview without editing it.

That afternoon I was walking out of The mom. I had big dark sunglasses, I hid my hair with a baseball cap, and popped my collar. I thought this would make it difficult for any paparazzi to recognize me. However she did and she stood in front of me with her cameraman and a microphone in hand.

"Leonardo, good afternoon, my name is Ariella Kaplan, from No Masks. Can I ask you a few questions?" She began

"Hi Ariella, sure, ask away" I say trying to smile as naturally as possible.

"We heard rumors that you are going to be the star of a controversial film, what can you tell us about that?"

"Look beautiful, I'm not sure how you guys manage to find out this information before we do. All I can say is and nothing is set in stone yet, my manager is still negotiating."

"Tell me about your plays in the theater. They have proved to be a huge success." She said smiling

"Fortunately for me, my fans are loyal and support me in everything I do. I am grateful from the bottom my heart…"

"Except when it comes to music" she says interrupting me, "everyone says that as an actor you're great but that music is not your thing. I imagine you won't be setting foot in another recording studio."

"You imagine wrong beautiful" I say trying not to show how upset her comment made me, "I will be recording another album and I assure you that I will be very successful in the music industry just like I am in acting."

"God willing" she replies seriously

"No, Leonardo is here to stay" I replied with some annoyance in my voice

"God willing, nothing is guaranteed in life you could die in a few days"

"Until I want to! I will live until I want to!" I say raising my voice

"Thank you for your time" she says in a calm voice, "we hope you continue being successful in what you do and that maybe you can give us an exclusive interview when you present your new album."

She turns her back to me and walked away.

That same night I saw the interview on television. It infuriated me, she made me look like an imbecile after repeating her absurd phrase, "God willing."

Seeing her walk into the restaurant, alone and with that confidence made me remember her words.

When our eyes met again I felt like she was telling me once again, "God willing."

"Leonardo? My goodness Leonardo wake up!!!" Aranzazu is now yelling

"Call the paramedics! I think the inaudible had a heart attack!" GL shouts

A heart attack? Who are they talking about? What you Leonardo had a heart attack?

Because I will not die until I want to!!!

HUG

I close my eyes as I tried to stifle the tears...I remember it all started on a Sunday night of October 16, 2005...

My mother had planned to travel to Mexico; we agreed that I would take her to the bus terminal because she does not like to travel by plane.

I came home after visiting friends at about 7:00PM and my mother was already outside with all her suitcases ready...

"Mother, why are you taking so many bags if you know that the bus won't allow more than 2? Also, all of that won't fit my car!"

"The thing is your brother, Vale, is going to take me in his minivan."

"Even so; there are far too many cases. You're going to need to leave some behind?" I insisted.

"No child, you don't understand, your brother Vale is coming to Mexico too." My mother replied.
"And what did Isela say?" I asked.

"She's also coming along with the children."

I saw my sister-in-law Isela going down the stairs with another suitcase in hand and she started loading everything in the minivan.

Inside the house were my father, my brother, my sister and my friend, Mary Juanjo.

The day before, I had just bought TV and called my brother inside to check on it. We were in my room when my sister-in-law came in and said:

"My love? The kids are already impatient."

"I want to get off, I want to get off!" Exclaimed my nephew, Brandon; he's 3 years old.

Once everyone was out of the house, we said goodbye. I hugged my brother Vale and then my mother.

"Be careful," My sister Mary said.

"Have a good trip," My friend Juanjo said.

"God be with you," My father said. "Remember you're carrying your life and four more in your hands."

Off they went on their way to Mexico…

On Monday night, while returning from work with my friend Juanjo, I said:

"You know what else is making me feel bad?"

"What is it?" Juanjo asked me.

"The night of their departure, I gave a hug to Vale and my mother but not Isela."

"And that bothered you? When they return next week, you give her all the hugs you want." Juanjo replied.

When we got home, my father was asleep because he had to get up at 5 AM for work. We had dinner and afterwards, we used my computer until about 3:00 AM. Since we were working the afternoon shift, We could sleep in. We said goodnight to each other and we went to our rooms. At about 5:20 AM, the phone rings…

Ring…ring…ring…ring…ring…

I was between dreams, more asleep than awake, I answered:

"Hello?"

"Uncle Benjamin? Sorry to wake you up at this hour," I recognized it the voice of my niece Lourdes, who lives in the village of California. "I just received news. There has been an accident in Mexico and your mother and aunt Edi were seriously injured…"

I jolted up from bed. I went to wake my friend Juanjo and said:

"Juanjo, we have to go to my father's job to tell him about what happened to Vale and the rest. They had an accident and I received news that my mother and Isela are in critical condition. He needs to go to Mexico."

I filled my father in regarding what happened. I went to see the supervisor and told him in English:

"There's been an emergency; my father needs to go to Mexico."

She gave her consent so my father went home. Once we arrived, I also phoned my other brothers, started arranging flights to Mexico. By 10 AM, we got news...

My brother Paco pulls over and parks on the roadside, crying, I parked the car beside his and he told me:

"I just spoke with someone in Mexico...Isela...has died..."

My brother was unharmed; as well as Brandon (the 3 yr old), and Jasmine, who was 1 year and 10 months.

My mother stayed long in the hospital, fighting for her life and thankfully made it...

I will always feel bad for not give her one last hug...my sister-in-law Isela (RIP).

TRUE LOVE

October 1949…

They'd gone to get water from the small water hole. Edi and her friend were having a conversation when herfriend says,

"Here comes Pancho Guillen."

Edi turned to see if it was true that Pancho was approaching; she saw that he turned and walked away…soon enough she realized why, Don Trino, Edi's father was around.

A few days later, Pancho had the opportunity and asked Edi, "Be my girlfriend?" She was a catechist and he asked that she teach him also.

She responded, "I have a boyfriend"

"End things with him and be my girlfriend" he replied

Edi asked him for a few days to contemplate on his proposal. She ended things with her boyfriend and began her romantic relationship with Pancho. They dated until March 1950…

Edi was asked by Pancho to marry him, Edi replied:

"First, I want us to complete the first 9 Sacred Heart Fridays together, to see if we should get married. I want you to confess and take communion every first Friday of the month and then see if it is right for us to get married."

Pancho said: "It's a long time, the life of a Christian."

Edi said: "Then do the first 5 Saturdays in honor of the Blessed Virgin."

Every first Saturday of the month for five months, Edi watched with glee that Pancho went to the temple to confess and to attend communion.

On Sunday, August 6, 1950, Pancho visited Edi's home to ask for Edi's hand from Silverio Calderon and Francisco Rodriguez.

Don Trino, very seriously asked:

"Is it true that you want to marry Pancho Guillen? You know whose son he is?"

Edi replied:

"He's the son of Don Antonino Guillén and Maria de Jesus Jaramillo who is reputed to be a holy woman…"

Her father then asks, "will you wait till the wedding date? Or are you planning on fleeing with him?"

"I'm waiting till the wedding date." She answers

The wedding date was set on Friday, March 30, 1951 at 8 PM. Pancho hadn't done military service before that, so he was prohibited from having a banquet wedding.

The wedding took place…The first night of their being married, Edi was dropped off in the house of Beatriz Guillén, her sister in law. The second night was spent at home with their parents, José Trinidad Corona and Bardomiana Zavala and finally, the third day of their marriage; they officially began their married life.

On Wednesday, July 16, 1952 came the first of the 12 children from this marriage…

The names of the 12 children are:

Jose Carmen
Jose Maria
Norberto
Bernardita
Nazario
Maria Refugio
Maria
Francisco
Juventino
Benjamin
Jose Trinidad
Jose Valentin.

On April 28, 2001 Monsignor Francis Gillganon celebrated the Golden wedding anniversary with them in the Parish of the Annunciation in Missouri and California.

On 2 April 2011, Bishop John Gaydos held the Diamond Wedding anniversary at St Peter in Jefferson City.

This marriage has more than 50 grandchildren and over 30 great-grandchildren…

This is a brief history of my parents. My mother continues to share her stories. My mother is a woman who despite her age and having sustained injuries from a serious accident in October 2005, retains a privileged memory.

I wanted to share with you their story as in the coming months; they will be celebrating their Platinum Wedding anniversary.

My parent's marriage is something to be proud of and I am privileged to be part of their family because marriages like theirs are very few. Their marriage looks, feels, and breathes of love and respect between two people as they live day by day; that's REAL LOVE!!!